The Knight
in Rusty Armor

The Knight
in Rusty Armor

為自己出征

燙金珍藏版

羅伯‧費雪 —— 著　王石珍 —— 譯

Contents

勇敢面對自己，就能找到喜歡的人生

勵志作家 **艾爾文**

　　如果這輩子要經歷很多的阻礙，我們要先學會突破的是「自我束縛」。

　　人一生會遇到很多的問題，有些很簡單，有些卻很複雜，要鼓起勇氣面對那些問題總是不容易。只是在走了那麼多的路、繞了那麼大的圈後，我才漸漸明瞭，即使問題再怎麼難以面對，最終都是在學習面對自己。

　　面對自己，就有能力找到喜歡的人生，而要學會面對，就要先練習接受。接受自己當下的樣子，接受目前生命所給予的挑戰，接受從來沒想過的難題，接受事情不會照自己的意願發展。如此一來，我們才能看清楚對我們真正重要的人事物，感受早已在身邊的各種幸福，學會看見自己身上的優點，學會不再因為缺點而到處躲躲藏藏。

　　很開心這世上存在這樣的一本書，用著簡單的故事解釋那些難懂的問題，邀請讀者陪著書中的武士一步一步地成長，也一步一步地更加認識自己。從征服城堡中的惡龍，到征服舊我、無知、恐懼；從救出公主，到救贖自己。最後脫下束縛自己好久的盔甲，以最喜歡的樣子面對世界，勇敢活著。

　　雖然，我並不是在人生最低潮時讀了這本書，但如果可以，我一定會把這本書送到當時那張桌子上。往後，如果再次遇到看似熟悉卻又陌生的迷茫時，我也會把這本書當成指南，檢視那時候的自己，提醒自己該往哪裡去。

　　無論你現在處在什麼樣的人生階段，遇到什麼樣的難題，我想這本書都能給你更多的力量。也許它不會直接告訴你答案，但它會讓你知道如何解答。試著拿起這本書閱讀，然後從現在開始──為自己出征，為自己感到驕傲。

放膽在童話中探險，重獲心靈自由

前臺灣大學哲學系教授 **傅佩榮**

　　如果不引述學派、不賣弄術語，只就每個人當下反省的心得來看，「自我」有三層面貌：一是外在的形象，由別人的眼光所見的自我綜合而成。二是自己內在的主觀認定，這種認定可能會受別人的影響，但是畢竟還有「自以為是」的成分。三是心靈深處的自我，這個自我與別人有相通的能力，甚至與宇宙萬物都可以產生共鳴。

　　我們平日生活，往往靠著外在我與內在我聯合起來，一起面對世界，經常忘記了真我或心靈我的存在，以至常有落寞的感受。得到的越多，失去的也越多。但是，平白無故要人認真對待心靈我，卻又有些困難。原因何在？在於生活只是由習慣在主導與重複，累積了一層層的心理防衛作用。雖然明知山下有塊石頭，等著我們日復一日的去推向山頂，我們還是像命運注定的薛西弗斯一樣，踩著沉重的步伐，走向大石。

防衛是為了保護，既定的命運雖然使人不耐，但是已知的一切總是較為熟悉的。何必去反抗？何必去突破？在黑暗中躍向彼岸，固然是勇敢的表現，但是真有彼岸嗎？換個方式來說，當我盡量擺脫外在我的束縛與壓力，並且辨明內在我的虛偽與自憐，然後呢？誰能保證一定可以獲得可貴的真我？並且，即使展現了真我，就一定可以得到快樂嗎？也許那種快樂與我現在所企求的快樂，是不同性質的，那麼，我如何確知自己一定會喜歡呢？

　　這一系列的問題應該都有合理的答案，但是關鍵在於：沒有人可以代替我自己回答。理論上的敘述與闡釋，有時更增加了困惑，學者專家的卓見在這些問題上是無能為力的。那麼，轉向寓言體裁求援吧！

　　以一種聽故事的心情，像小孩子在童話世界中從事心靈探險一般，我打開了《為自己出征》這本小書；一口氣念完整篇故事，但是並沒有隨手丟開，卻有了再念一遍的衝動。念了第三遍時，才能且讀且想，綜合提出一些心得。

　　故事的主角是一位武士，整天穿戴盔甲，到處去救人。他想證明自己是「心地好、善良、充滿愛心」的人。久而久之，他的妻子與兒子都看不到他盔甲下的真面目，他自己也忘了自己的長相，問題十分嚴重。他決心脫掉盔甲，到森林去請教法師。

我們在人間，常以外在我的表現來決定內在我的性質，進而根本遺忘了心靈我。人生的過程，無異於自我遺忘的過程，等到察覺困境，往往已是中午階段了。那麼，如何找回自我呢？法師讓松鼠、鴿子扮演嚮導，暗示武士，大自然的啟發是值得參考的；不過，解決困難仍然要靠自己。他必須通過三座城堡：沉默之堡、知識之堡、志勇之堡。

顧名思義，人在「沉默」中，必須面對自我。當外在的噪雜平息時，內心的茫然不安浮現了。如果用心，不難聽到真我的聲音，真我提醒自己什麼是真正值得的目標。武士為此痛哭流涕，淚水卻腐蝕融化了頭盔，他的頭部不再受拘束了。

「知識」是大家可以分享的，但是若無自知之明，博學又有何益？如果無法認清「需要不等於愛」，也就不能以適當態度與人相處。需要是一回事，愛是另一回事，需要可多可少，愛卻永遠是人人珍惜的。像這種正確的知識，就會帶人走向愛之道。

「志勇」是指志氣與勇氣，用以克服疑懼之意。人生不能沒有疑懼，最大的疑懼正是喪失自我的立足之地。不過，越是如此，越容易受制於疑懼。唯有無私忘我，有如「置之死地而後生」，才能擁有真正的自我。

　　經過這三座城堡，武士身上的盔甲全部掉落，重新得到自由的生命。我們是否也能經由沉默、知識與志勇，擺脫外在我的束縛，調整內在我的成見，讓心靈我自由展現，活出一個有愛的人生呢？這是每一個人的挑戰。

武士的難題

The Knight's Dilemma

The Knight's Dilemma

Once a long time ago, in a land far away, there lived a knight who thought of himself as good, kind, and loving. He did all the things that good, kind, and loving knights do. He fought foes who were bad, mean, and hateful. He slew dragons and rescued fair damsels in distress. When the knight business was slow, he had the annoying habit of rescuing damsels even if they did not want to be rescued, so, although many ladies were grateful to him, just as many were furious with him. This he accepted philosophically. After all, one can't please everybody.

This knight was famous for his armor. It reflected such bright rays of light that villagers would swear they had seen the sun rise in the north or set in the east when the knight rode off to battle. And he rode off to battle frequently. At the mere mention of a crusade, the knight would eagerly don his shining armor, mount his horse, and ride off in any direction. So eager was he, in fact, that sometimes he would ride off in several directions at once, which was no easy feat.

武士的難題

　　很久很久以前，在遙遠的地方，有一位武士，他認為自己心地好、善良，而且充滿了愛。他要做所有心地好、善良、充滿了愛的武士會做的事，向一切心地壞、卑鄙又可惡的武士挑戰。他屠龍，也拯救遇難的公主，不過當武士這門生意比較清淡的時候，他有個讓人討厭的習慣，就是主動去搭救美麗公主，不管她們需不需要拯救。因此，雖然有很多公主感激這個武士，但也有一樣多的公主覺得他很「機車」。對於這一點，他很哲學性地接受了──畢竟要討好每一個人是不可能的。

　　可是，真正讓這個武士聲名大噪的還是他的盔甲。這套盔甲是國王賞賜的禮物，是用一種非常稀有、和太陽一樣閃亮的金屬所製成的。有些村民發誓，他們曾經看見太陽從北邊升起，或從東邊落下。事實上，他們看到的不過是武士朝著四面八方前進而已。只要一提到任務，武士馬上會套上盔甲，跳上馬，向任何可能的方向騎過去。有時候，他會弄得同時朝幾個不同的方向前

For years this knight strove to be the number one knight in all the kingdom. There was always another battle to be won, dragon to be slain, or damsel to be rescued.

The knight had a faithful and somewhat tolerant wife, Juliet, who wrote beautiful poetry, said clever things, and had a penchant for wine. He also had a young, golden-haired son, Christopher, who he hoped would grow up to be a courageous knight.

Juliet and Christopher saw little of the knight, because when not fighting battles, slaying dragons, and rescuing damsels, he was occupied with trying on his armor and admiring its brilliance. As time went on, the knight became so enamored of his armor that he began wearing it to dinner and often to bed. After a time, he didn't bother to take it off at all. Gradually his family forgot how he looked without it.

Occasionally, Christopher would ask his mother what his father looked like. When this happened, Juliet would lead the boy to the fireplace and point above it to a portrait of the knight. "There's your father," she would sigh.

One afternoon, while contemplating the portrait, Christopher said to his mother, "I wish I could see Father in person."

"You can't have everything!" snapped Juliet. She was growing impatient

進，這可真不是件容易的差事。

許多年來，武士拚了命要變成天下排名第一的武士，所以總是有打不完的仗、殺不完的龍，和拯救不完的公主。

武士有個忠心耿耿又心胸寬大的老婆——茉莉亞。茉莉亞會寫美美的詩、說聰明的話，對酒又很有品味，另外還有個希望將來能繼承家業的金髮美少年兒子，克斯。

茉莉亞和克斯很少有時間真的和武士相處，因為他不是在打仗、屠龍、拯救公主，就是穿著盔甲顧影自憐。說真的，武士愛他的盔甲愛到不願意脫掉的地步。吃晚飯，他穿著盔甲；和朋友在一起，他穿著盔甲；甚至上床，他也穿著盔甲；終於有一天，他的家人和朋友都忘了他不穿盔甲是什麼樣子。

偶爾，克斯會問他媽媽：「爸爸究竟長什麼樣子？」然後，茉莉亞會帶她的兒子到壁爐旁邊，指著一幅武士的畫像，嘆著氣說：「這就是你爸爸的長相。」「至少，這是他從前長的樣子。」

有天下午，克斯看著畫像，對他媽媽說：「我希望能看到真正的爸爸。」

「你不能什麼都要！」他媽媽大聲地罵他。她的心情也不

with having only a painting to remind her of her husband's face, and she was tired from having her sleep disturbed by the clanking of armor.

When he was at home and not completely preoccupied with his armor, the knight usually delivered monologues on his exploits. Juliet and Christopher were seldom able to get a word in edgewise. When they did, the knight shut it out either by closing his visor or by abruptly going to sleep.

One day, Juliet confronted her husband. "I think you love your armor more than you love me."

"That's not true," answered the knight. "Didn't I love you enough to rescue you from that dragon and set you up in this classy castle with wall-to-wall stones?"

"What you loved," said Juliet, peering through his visor so that she could see his eyes, "was the idea of rescuing me. You didn't really love me then, and you don't really love me now."

"I do love you," insisted the knight, hugging her clumsily in his cold, stiff armor and nearly breaking her ribs.

"Then take off that armor so that I can see who you really are!" she demanded.

"I can't take it off. I have to be ready to mount my horse and ride off in

好，因為只有一幅畫能提醒她老公的長相，而且她又總是睡不安穩，因為武士整晚在盔甲裡翻來覆去，軋軋作響。

而且就算在家，沒有穿著盔甲顧影自憐的時候，武士通常都在滔滔不絕地誇耀自己過去的光榮事蹟。茱莉亞和克斯連話題的邊都接不上，就算有幾次不小心接上了話題，武士不是馬上關上面盔，就是突然說他要上床睡覺了。

有一天，茱莉亞終於和她老公攤牌：「我覺得，你愛盔甲甚過於愛我。」

「這不是真的。」武士回答：「我不是把妳從那隻惡龍的魔爪裡拯救出來，又把妳安頓在這麼高級的城堡裡嗎？」

茱莉亞用力從他的面盔裡看進去，好看到他的眼睛，她說：「你喜歡的，只是去拯救我而已，你當初沒有真正愛過我，現在也不是真正愛我。」

「我真的愛妳。」武士堅持，笨拙地用冰冷又堅硬的盔甲擁抱她，差點把她的肋骨都弄斷了。

「那麼，你把這件鐵衣脫掉，好讓我看到真正的你。」她命令他。

「可是我得隨時準備好，跳上我的馬，朝四面八方騎過去

any direction," explained the knight.

"If you don't take off that armor, I'm taking Christopher, getting on my horse, and riding out of your life."

Well, this was a real blow to the knight. He didn't want Juliet to leave. He loved his wife and his son and his classy castle, but he also loved his armor because it showed everyone who he was — a good, kind, and loving knight. Why didn't Juliet realize that he was any of these things?

The knight was in turmoil. Finally he came to a decision. Continuing to wear the armor wasn't worth losing Juliet and Christopher.

Reluctantly, the knight reached up to remove his helmet, but it didn't budge! He pulled harder. It held fast. Dismayed, he tried lifting his visor but, alas, that was stuck, too. Though he tugged on the visor again and again, nothing happened.

The knight paced back and forth in great agitation. How could this have happened? Perhaps it was not so surprising to find the helmet stuck since he had not removed it for years, but the visor was another matter. He had opened it regularly to eat and drink. Why, he had lifted it just that morning over a breakfast of scrambled eggs and suckling pig.

Suddenly the knight had an idea. Without saying where he was going,

啊！」

「如果你不把這件鬼東西脫下來，我就要帶著兒子，騎上馬，馬上離開你。」

對武士來說，這可是個嚴重的打擊。他不願意茱莉亞離開他，他愛他的太太、他的兒子、和他鋪滿石磚的高級城堡，但是他也愛他的盔甲，因為，他的盔甲向每一個人展示他是個什麼樣的人——一個心地好、善良、充滿了愛的武士。他非常意外太太並不認為他心地好、善良，而且充滿了愛。

有這麼一陣子，武士真是五內如焚，最後他終於下了決定，如果繼續穿著盔甲意味著他會失去茱莉亞和克斯，那他寧可脫掉盔甲。

武士不情願地伸出手想取下頭盔，卻意外發現頭盔一動也不動。他再用力地拉，可是還是不能把頭盔拉下來。驚慌之下，他試著把頭盔上的面盔抬起來，但是面盔也卡住了。他一遍又一遍地用力扯，然而面盔仍然文風不動。

心煩意亂的武士不停地走來走去。這怎麼可能呢？頭盔卡住不奇怪，因為他已經好多年沒有脫下頭盔了。可是面盔又是另外一回事，他一直不斷把面盔打開，吃吃喝喝。事實上就在當天

he hurried to the blacksmith's shop in the castle courtyard. When he arrived, the smith was shaping a horseshoe with his bare hands.

"Smith," said the knight, "I have a problem."

"You are a problem, sire," quipped the smith with his usual tact.

The knight, who normally enjoyed bantering, glowered. "I'm in no mood for your wisecracks right now. I'm stuck in this armor," he bellowed as he stamped his steel-clad foot, accidentally bringing it down on the smith's big toe.

The smith let out a howl and, momentarily forgetting the knight was his master, dealt him a smashing blow to the helmet. The knight felt only a twinge of discomfort. The helmet didn't budge.

"Try again," ordered the knight, unaware that the smith obliged him out of anger.

"With pleasure," the smith agreed, swinging a nearby hammer with vengeance and bringing it down squarely on the knight's helmet. The blow didn't even make a dent.

The knight was distraught. The smith was by far the strongest man in the kingdom. If he couldn't shuck the knight out of his armor, who could?

Being a kind man, except when his big toe was crushed, the smith

早上，他還把面盔抬起，吃炒蛋和乳豬當早餐呢！

武士突然有了個主意，沒說要去哪裡，就衝進了城堡院子的鐵匠鋪裡。到的時候，鐵匠正在赤手空拳地拉扯著馬蹄鐵。

「鐵匠，」武士說：「我有個問題。」

「大人，你就是個問題。」鐵匠伶牙俐齒地回應他。

通常很能欣賞這種哲學式妙語的武士，面紅耳赤地看著鐵匠：「我現在沒心情聽你的俏皮話，我給困在這件盔甲裡了。」他邊說邊用力頓著腳，一不留神，就踩到了鐵匠的大腳趾。

鐵匠發出一聲痛苦的大叫，忘了武士是主人，朝他的頭盔重重地打了一拳，武士只感覺到一點點不舒服的感覺，但是頭盔動也不動。

「再試一次！」武士命令他，完全沒有感覺到鐵匠是因為憤怒才順從他。

「樂意得很。」鐵匠說。順手舉起一把斧頭，猛力地朝武士的頭盔砍了過去，結果頭盔上連個凹痕都沒有砍出來。

武士覺得一陣驚慌，鐵匠是全國最強壯的人，如果連他都不能把他的盔甲剝下來，那麼誰能？

除了大腳趾頭被踩到的時候之外，鐵匠基本上是個好人，

sensed the knight's panic and grew sympathetic. "You have a tough plight, Knight, but don't give up. Come back tomorrow after I'm rested. You caught me at the end of a hard day."

Dinner time that evening was difficult. Juliet became increasingly annoyed as she pushed bits of food she had mashed through the holes in the knight's visor. Partway through the meal, the knight told Juliet that the blacksmith had tried to split open the armor but had failed.

"I don't believe you, you clanking clod!" she shouted, as she smashed her half-full plate of pigeon stew on his helmet.

The knight felt nothing. Only when gravy began dripping down past the eyeholes in his visor did he realize that he'd been hit on the head. He had barely felt the smith's hammer that afternoon either. In fact, when he thought about it, his armor kept him from feeling much of anything, and he had worn it for so long now that he'd forgotten how things felt without it.

The knight was upset that Juliet didn't believe he was trying to get his armor off. He and the smith had tried, and they kept at it for many more days without success. Each day the knight grew more despondent and Juliet grew colder. Finally, the knight had to admit that the smith's efforts were useless. "Strongest man in the kingdom, indeed! You can't even break open this steel

他感覺到武士的驚慌，開始同情起他來。「大人，你這下麻煩大了，不過別放棄，明天，等我休息夠了你再來，我今天累了一天，沒力氣了。」

當天晚上吃飯真是個大挑戰，茱莉亞把小塊的食物弄碎，塞進武士面盔的時候火氣變得越來越大。吃到一半，武士告訴茱莉亞，鐵匠想幫他把盔甲弄下來，不過沒有成功。

「我不相信你，你這個亂搖亂響的粗人。」她大叫，一邊把半盤的燉鴿子摔在武士的頭盔上。

武士一點感覺也沒有，只有在肉汁從面盔的眼洞裡滴進去的時候，他才知道有東西打到了他的頭，就像下午他也不知道鐵匠在敲他的頭一樣。其實回想起來，他的盔甲讓他變得沒感覺，穿盔甲穿了這麼久，他已經忘了不穿盔甲的感受了。

武士覺得很沮喪，因為茱莉亞不相信他的確想把盔甲脫掉。他和鐵匠試了好幾天，但總是不成功。一天天過去，他變得越來越痛苦，茱莉亞變得越來越冷淡。最後武士只好承認鐵匠的努力是沒用的：「全國最強壯的人，騙誰？連這件鐵做的垃圾也敲不爛！」武士絕望地大喊著。

junkyard!" the knight yelled in frustration.

When the knight returned home, Juliet shrieked at him, "Your son has nothing but a portrait for a father, and I'm tired of talking to a closed visor. I'm never pushing food through the holes of that wretched thing again. I've mashed my very last mutton chop!"

"It's not my fault that I got stuck in this armor. I had to wear it so that I would always be ready for battle. How else could I get nice castles and horses for you and Christopher?"

"You didn't do it for us, You did it for yourself!" argued Juliet.

The knight was sick at heart that his wife didn't seem to love him anymore. He also feared that if he didn't get his armor off soon, Juliet and Christopher would really leave. He had to get the armor off, but he didn't know how to do it.

The knight dismissed one idea after another as being unlikely to work. Some of the plans were downright dangerous. He knew that any knight who would even think of melting his armor off with a castle torch, freezing it off by jumping into an icy moat, or blasting it off with a cannon was badly in need of help. Unable to find aid in his own kingdom, the knight decided to search in other lands. Somewhere there must be someone who can help me get this

武士回家的時候，茱莉亞向他大叫：「你的兒子只剩下一幅爸爸的畫像，我再也不要跟一個關上的面盔說話，你也別想我會再朝那個鬼東西的洞裡塞東西給你吃，上次的羊排就是你的最後一道菜了。」

　　「給關在盔甲裡也不是我的錯，我穿著盔甲是因為隨時要去打仗啊！不然我怎麼能夠為妳和克斯賺到這麼高級的城堡和馬匹？」

　　「你才不是為我們做的，你是為自己做的！」茱莉亞反駁他。

　　武士心灰意冷，因為茱莉亞不再愛他了，他也害怕如果他不把盔甲脫下的話，茱莉亞和克斯一定真的會離開他，他一定得把盔甲弄掉，只是不知道怎麼做。

　　武士想了一個又一個的主意，可是沒有一個行得通，例如他知道有些武士會想到用城堡的火炬把盔甲燒熔掉；有些會說跳進冰封的護城河裡，讓冰塊把盔甲冰裂掉；最不濟還可以用大砲，不過這些主意實在都太危險了。在自己的王國得不到幫助，武士決定要到別的地方試試運氣，某個地方總會有個人能夠幫他把這件盔甲弄下來。

armor off, he thought.

Of course, he would miss Juliet, Christopher, and his classy castle. He also feared that in his absence Juliet might find love with another knight, one willing to remove his armor at bedtime and to be more of a father to Christopher. Nevertheless, the knight had to go, so, early one morning, he got onto his horse, and he rode away. He didn't dare look back for fear he might change his mind.

On his way out of the province, the knight stopped to say goodbye to the king, who had been very good to him. The king lived in a grand castle atop a hill in the high-rent district. As the knight rode across the drawbridge and into the courtyard, he saw the court jester sitting cross-legged, playing a reed flute.

The jester was called Gladbag because, over his shoulder, he carried a beautiful rainbow-colored bag filled with all sorts of things that made people laugh or smile. There were strange cards that he used to tell people's fortunes, brightly colored beads that he made appear and disappear, and funny little puppets that he used to amusingly insult his audiences.

"Hi, Gladbag," said the knight. "I came to say farewell to the king."

The jester looked up.

當然，他會想念茱莉亞、克斯，和他的高級城堡，他也害怕在他不在的時候茱莉亞可能會愛上另一個武士，這個武士願意在上床的時候把盔甲脫下來，也願意做克斯的爸爸。不論如何，武士都得要走，所以，有一天清晨，他騎上馬離開家，走的時候連頭也不敢回，怕自己會改變心意。

要離開王國的時候，武士決定順路去和國王說個再見，畢竟國王一向待他不薄。國王住在山頂高級住宅區的豪華城堡裡。武士通過城堡吊橋，騎馬進院子時，看到宮廷小丑盤著腿坐著，一邊吹著蘆笛。

這個宮廷小丑叫作樂包，因為他總是在肩膀上背著一個像彩虹般美麗的包包，裡面裝滿著各式各樣讓人們開心的小玩意兒，有奇怪的算命牌，有能夠隱形的彩色珠珠，還有用來戲弄觀眾的有趣小玩偶。

「喂，樂包，」武士說：「我來和國王道別。」

樂包抬頭望著他說：

「國王起床就遠行，

"The king has up and gone away.

To you there's nothing he can say."

"Where has he gone?" asked the knight.

"He's taken off on a new crusade.

If you wait for him, you'll be delayed."

The knight was disappointed that he had missed the king and perturbed that he couldn't join him on the crusade. "Oh," he sighed, "I could starve to death in this armor by the time the king returns. I might never see him again." The knight felt very much like slumping in his saddle, but, of course, his armor wouldn't let him.

"Well, aren't you a silly sight?

All your might can't solve your plight."

"I'm in no mood for your insulting rhymes," barked the knight, stiffening in his armor. "Can't you take someone's problem seriously for once?"

In a clear, lyrical voice, Gladbag sang:

"Problems never set me a-rockin.

They're opportunities a-knockin."

"You'd sing a different tune if you were the one stuck in here," growled

於你他也無話應。」

「他去哪裡了？」武士問。

樂包回答：

「國王前去打聖戰，

切莫遲疑快追趕。」

和國王失之交臂，又不能參加聖戰的行列，讓武士覺得非常失望。他嘆了一口氣：「國王回來的時候，我可能已經在盔甲裡餓死，可能我們再也見不到面了。」武士真想在馬鞍上頹然倒下，不過，穿著盔甲當然是做不到的。

然後，樂包說：

「你看來受苦已久，

雖神勇不能自救。」

「我才不要在這裡忍受你侮辱人的兒歌。」武士生氣地說，在盔甲裡挺直：「你就不能對別人的事認真一點嗎？」

用清澈、吟詩般的聲音，樂包唱道：

「問題不能困擾我，

機會來時要掌握。」

「如果你也卡在這裡的話，你就會唱另一種調子了。」武

the knight.

Gladbag retorted:

"We're all stuck in armor of a kind.

Yours is merely easier to find."

"I don't have time to stay and listen to your nonsense. I have to find a way to get out of this armor." With that, the knight kneed his mount forward to leave, but Gladbag called after him:

"There is one who can help you. Knight,

to bring the real you into sight."

The knight pulled his horse to a stop and, excitedly, he turned back to Gladbag. "You know someone who can get me out of this armor? Who is it?"

"Merlin the Magician you must see.

Then you'll discover how to be free."

"Merlin? The only Merlin I've ever heard of is the great and wise teacher of King Arthur."

"Yes, yes, that's his claim to fame.

This Merlin I know is one and the same."

"But it can't be!" exclaimed the knight. "Merlin and Arthur lived long ago."

士更生氣地説。

　　樂包反駁他：

　　「同樣盔甲在吾身，

　　爾之牢籠容易見。」

　　「我沒時間聽你的廢話，我得設法把自己從這身盔甲裡弄出來。」説完，武士用膝蓋頂著馬，催馬前進。樂包從後面喊：

　　「有人能夠幫助你，

　　助你真我出廢墟。」

　　武士拉著馬，向樂包轉了回去，興奮地問：「你知道有人能把我從盔甲裡解救出來？是誰？」

　　「梅林法師是其名，見他你將得新生。」（注：英國中古時期傳説中，梅林是個偉大的魔術師，亞瑟王的老師，幫助亞瑟王登上國王寶座。）

　　「梅林？」武士問：「我聽過唯一的梅林，就是亞瑟王偉大的明師。」（注：相傳亞瑟王為英國中古時期偉大的明君，出身低微，因拔出「石中劍」而成英國國王，創「圓桌武士」。）

　　「成名之道緣於此，

　　梅林就是亞瑟師。」

　　「但是，不可能！」武士説：「梅林和亞瑟是古時候的人

Gladbag replied:

"It's true, yet he's alive and well.

In yonder woods the sage doth dwell."

"But those woods are so big," said the knight. "How will I find him in there?"

Gladbag smiled.

"One never knows be it days, weeks, or years,

when the pupil is ready, the teacher appears."

"I can't wait for Merlin to show up. I'm going to look for him" said the knight. He reached out and shook Gladbag's hand in gratitude, nearly crushing the jester's fingers with his gauntlet.

Gladbag yelped. The knight quickly released the jester's hand. "Sorry." Gladbag rubbed his bruised fingers.

"When the armor's gone from you,

you'll feel the pain of others, too."

"I'm off!" said the knight. He wheeled his horse around, and with new hope in his heart, galloped away to find Merlin.

了。」

樂包回答：

「梅林活著，活得好，

遠方樹林大師找。」

「可是，那些樹林這麼大，」武士說：「我怎麼找得到他？」

樂包笑了：

「無人知，不論何時，

徒弟來，老師就到。」

「我可不能等梅林自己出現，我要去找他。」他伸出手，感謝地握著樂包的手，鐵手套差點捏斷了樂包的手指頭。

樂包痛得大叫起來，武士很快地鬆開手指，說：「對不起。」

樂包揉著他瘀青的手指：

「來年盔甲離你時，他人痛苦身受日。」

「出發！」武士說，他拉著馬頭，轉了個方向，心中充滿新希望，尋找梅林大師去了。

梅林樹林

In Merlin's Woods

In Merlin's Woods

It was no easy task to find the wily wizard. There were many woods to search but only one Merlin. So the poor knight rode on, day after day, night after night, becoming weaker and weaker.

As he rode through the woods alone, the knight realized there were many things he didn't know. He'd always thought of himself as very smart, but he didn't feel very smart at all trying to survive in the woods.

Reluctantly he admitted to himself that he didn't even know the poisonous berries from the edible ones. This made eating a game of Russian roulette. Drinking was no less hazardous. The knight tried sticking his head into a stream, but his helmet filled up with water. Twice, he almost drowned. As if that weren't bad enough, he had been lost since entering the woods. The knight couldn't tell north from south or east from west. Fortunately, his horse could.

After months of searching in vain, the knight was quite discouraged. He still hadn't found Merlin even though he'd traveled many leagues. What

梅林樹林

想要找到這位智慧的大法師不是件簡單的事，樹林有很多，梅林只有一名。所以武士不停地向前騎，日以繼夜，同時也變得越來越虛弱。

獨自一個人騎馬穿過無數的樹林以後，武士得到一個結論——他其實不是什麼都懂。以前他一直認為自己很聰明。現在，千方百計地想在樹林裡活下去，他覺得自己真笨得可以。

雖然不情願，但他必須承認，他甚至不知道哪種莓子有毒，哪種可以吃。每次吃莓子都像在玩俄羅斯輪盤。喝水稍微不那麼危險，他可以把頭放進小溪裡喝水，可是頭盔裡充滿了水，有兩次他都差一點給淹死。這還不是最糟的，自從進了樹林以後他就迷路了，完全分不清東西南北，幸好他的馬比他有方向感得多。

過了好幾個月這種大海撈針的日子，武士簡直心灰意冷，即使他已經走了好多里格的路，他還是沒有找到梅林。更令人沮

made him feel worse was the fact that he didn't even know how far a league was.

One morning, he woke up feeling weaker than usual and a little peculiar. That was the morning he found Merlin. The knight recognized the magician at once. He was sitting under a tree, clothed in a long white robe. Animals of the forest were gathered around him, and birds were perched on his shoulders and arms.

The knight shook his head glumly from side to side, his armor squeaking as he did. How could all these animals find Merlin so easily when it was so hard for me?

Wearily, the knight climbed down from his horse "I've been looking for you," he said to the magician. "I've been lost for months."

"All your life," corrected Merlin, biting off a piece of carrot and sharing it with the nearest rabbit.

The knight stiffened. "I didn't come all this way to be insulted."

"Perhaps you have always taken the truth to be an insult," said Merlin, sharing the carrot with some of the other animals.

The knight didn't much like this remark either, but he was too weak from hunger and thirst to climb back on his horse and ride away. Instead,

喪的是，他甚至不曉得一里格有多遠。（注：一里格約四點八公里。）

有天早上，他醒了過來，覺得虛弱之外，還有一點奇怪的感覺。就在那天，他找到了梅林，睿智的大法師，武士馬上就認出他來。梅林坐在一棵樹下，穿著一件長長的白袍子，林子裡的動物圍在他的身旁，鳥兒棲息在他的肩膀和手臂上。

武士悶悶不樂地搖搖頭，他的盔甲發出一陣聲響，為什麼動物這麼容易就可以找到梅林，而他卻要這麼辛苦？

他疲倦地從馬上爬下來。「我到處在找你，」武士說：「我迷路迷了好幾個月。」

「其實是一輩子。」梅林糾正他，又咬下一塊紅蘿蔔，遞給身旁的兔子。

武士馬上變得很僵硬：「我不是來這裡受你侮辱的。」

「也許你一直覺得，事情的真相是個侮辱。」梅林說著，同時把紅蘿蔔再分給其他的動物吃。

武士也不喜歡這句話，可是，他又餓又渴，非常虛弱，沒辦法騎上馬離開，相反的，他那金屬包裹的身子摔倒在草地上。梅林同情地看了他一眼：「你真幸運，你太虛弱了，不能逃

he dropped his metal-encased body onto the grass. Merlin looked at him compassionately. "You are most fortunate," he commented. "You are too weak to run."

"What does that mean?" snapped the knight.

Merlin smiled in reply. "A person cannot run and also learn. He must stay in one place for a while."

"I'm going to stay here only long enough to learn how to get out of this armor," said the knight.

"When you learn that," stated Merlin, "you will never again have to climb on your horse and ride off in all directions."

The knight was too tired to question this. Somehow, he felt comforted and fell promptly asleep.

When the knight awakened, he saw Merlin and the animals all around him. He tried to sit up, but he was too weak. Merlin held out a silver cup with a strange-colored liquid in it. "Drink this," he ordered.

"What is it?" asked the knight, eyeing the cup suspiciously.

"You are so afraid," said Merlin. "Of course, that is why you put on the armor in the first place."

The knight didn't bother to deny this, for he was too thirsty.

走。」

「這是什麼意思？」武士厲聲叫道。

梅林微笑著：「人不能邊跑邊學，一定要在一個地方停留一會兒。」

武士軟化了下來：「我只要學會怎麼從這套盔甲裡出來，我就走。」

「等到你學會了，」梅林建議：「你就再也不用上馬，朝四面八方前進了。」

武士累到不能問為什麼，可是他覺得安心，所以馬上就睡著了。

醒來以後，動物和梅林圍在他身邊，他想坐起來，卻因為太虛弱而坐不起來。梅林遞給他一只銀杯，裡面裝滿了顏色古怪的液體。「喝下去。」梅林命令他。

「這是什麼？」武士問，懷疑地看著杯子裡的東西。

「你這麼害怕，」梅林說：「不過，當然，這就是當初為什麼你會穿上這身盔甲的原因。」

武士不想否認，因為他實在太渴了。

"All right, I'll drink it. Pour it into my visor."

"I will not," Merlin said. "It is too precious to waste. "He plucked a reed, put one end in the cup, and slipped the other into one of the holes in the knight's visor.

"This is a great idea!" said the knight.

"I call it a straw," replied Merlin.

"Why?"

Why not?"

The knight shrugged and sipped the liquid through the reed. The first sips seemed bitter, the later ones more pleasant, and the last swallows quite delicious. Grateful, the knight handed the cup back to Merlin. "You should put that stuff on the market. You could sell flagons of it."

Merlin just smiled.

"What is it?" asked the knight.

"Life," Merlin replied.

"Life?"

"Yes," said the wise magician. "Did it not first seem bitter, then, as you tasted more of it, was it not pleasant?"

The knight nodded. "Yes, and the last swallows were quite delicious."

「好吧，我喝，倒進我的面盔裡吧。」

「沒這回事，」梅林說：「這杯東西太珍貴了，不能浪費。」他掰斷了一根蘆草，把一頭放進杯裡，另一頭塞進武士面盔的洞裡。

「這個主意真不錯。」武士說。

「我叫它吸管。」梅林回答。

「為什麼？」

「為什麼不？」

武士點著頭，吸著液體，第一口好像有點苦，接下來卻越來越好喝，最後一口更是可口。

武士充滿感激地把杯子遞還給梅林：「你應該把這個東西拿到市場上去賣，一定可以大撈一筆。」

梅林只是微笑著。

「這是什麼？」武士問。

「生命。」梅林回答。

「生命？」

「對，」大師說：「剛開始有點苦，等到喝了幾口以後，是不是變得很可口？」

"That was when you began to accept what you were drinking."

"Are you saying that life is good when you accept it?" asked the knight.

"Is it not?" replied Merlin, raising an eyebrow in amusement.

"Do you expect me to accept all this heavy armor?"

"Ah," said Merlin, "you were not born with that armor. You put it on yourself. Have you ever asked yourself why?"

"Why not?"retorted the knight irritably. At this point, his head was beginning to hurt. He wasn't used to thinking in this manner.

"You will be able to think more clearly when you regain your strength," Merlin said.

With that, the magician clapped his hands, and the squirrels, holding nuts in their little mouths, lined up in front of the knight. Each squirrel climbed up onto the knight's shoulder, cracked and chewed a nut, then pushed the pieces through the knight's visor. The rabbits did the same thing with carrots, and the deer crushed roots and berries for the knight to eat. This method of feeding would never be endorsed by the health department, but what else could a knight who was stuck in his armor in the woods possibly do?

The animals fed the knight regularly, and Merlin gave him large cups of

武士點著頭：「對，而且最後的那幾口真是美味。」

「那是因為你開始接受了你在喝的東西。」

「你的意思是說，接受了生命的時候，生命其實是美好的？」武士問。

「不是嗎？」梅林回答，好玩地揚起一邊的眉毛。

「你是要我接受這麼重的盔甲嗎？」

「哦，」梅林說：「你不是生下來就穿著盔甲的，這是你自己穿上的。好，你有沒有問過自己為什麼要穿上盔甲呢？」

「為什麼不？」武士說，有一點生氣，他的頭開始痛，他不習慣這樣思考。

「等到你復元的時候，你就可以想得更清楚。」梅林說。

然後法師拍拍手，一隻隻含著堅果的松鼠，就排列在武士面前。每隻松鼠輪流爬到武士的肩膀上，把堅果敲碎、咬爛，再從他的面盔裡推進去。兔子餵他吃咬爛的紅蘿蔔，鹿則為他碾碎根莖食物和野莓子。這種餵食的方法一定不會被衛生署批准。可是，如果你在樹林裡，又給關在一套盔甲裡面，你還能怎麼辦呢？

每天，動物用這種方法餵武士吃東西，梅林則用吸管給他

Life to drink through the straw. Slowly the knight grew stronger, and he began to feel more hopeful.

Each day, he asked Merlin the same question: "When will I get out of this armor?" Each day, Merlin replied, "Patience! You have been wearing that armor for a long time. You cannot get out of it just like that."

One night, the animals and the knight were listening to the magician play the latest troubadour hits on his lute. Waiting until Merlin had finished playing "Hark Ye the Days of Old, When Knights Were Bold and Maidens Were Cold," the knight asked a question long on his mind. "Were you really the teacher of King Arthur?"

The magician's face lit up. "Yes, I taught Arthur," he said.

"But how can you still be alive? Arthur lived eons ago!" exclaimed the knight.

"Past, present, and future are all one when you are connected to the Source," replied Merlin.

"What is the Source?" asked the knight.

"It is the mysterious, invisible power that is the origin of all."

"I don't understand," said the knight.

"That is because you are trying to understand with your mind, but your

大杯的「生命」喝。慢慢的，武士開始有了力氣，並且充滿了新希望。

　　每天，他都會問梅林同樣的問題：「我什麼時候才能把這套盔甲丟掉？」每天，梅林都會回答：「你要忍耐，穿了這麼久，不可能這麼簡單就脫得下來。」

　　有一天晚上，動物和武士圍著梅林，聽他用魯特琴彈奏抒情的歌謠，武士決定問梅林一件他一直在想的事。等梅林彈完了那首〈武士懷舊〉，他問梅林：「你真的是亞瑟王的老師嗎？」

　　法師的臉亮了起來：「是的，我教過亞瑟。」他說。

　　「你怎麼可能現在還活著？那是很久以前的事了。」武士大叫。

　　「當你和原力相連接的時候，過去、現在和未來，是一體的。」梅林回答。

　　「什麼是原力？」武士問道

　　「原力是萬物之源，那股神祕又看不見的力量。」

　　「我不懂。」武士說。

　　「那是因為你想用腦子來了解，可是腦子是有限的。」

mind is limited."

"I have a very good mind," argued the knight.

"And a clever one," added Merlin. "It trapped you in all that armor."

The knight could not refute this. Then he remembered something that Merlin had said to him when he first arrived. "You once said that I put on this armor because I was afraid."

"Is that not true?" responded Merlin.

"No, I wore it for protection when I went to battle."

"And you were afraid you would be seriously hurt or killed," added Merlin.

"Isn't everybody?"

Merlin shook his head. "Who ever said you had to go to battle?"

"I had to prove that I was a good, kind, and loving knight."

"If you really were good, kind, and loving, why did you have to prove it?" Merlin asked.

The knight escaped thinking about this in his usual manner of escaping things – he drifted off to sleep.

The following morning, he awakened with an odd thought stuck in his mind: Was it possible that he was not good, kind, and loving? He decided to

「可是我的腦筋很好。」武士說。

「而且還很聰明，」梅林加上一句：「就是腦子把你困在這套盔甲裡面。」

武士沒辦法反駁這點。然後，他想到剛來的時候，梅林跟他說的話：「有一次你說，我是因為害怕才穿上這身盔甲的。」

「難道不是嗎？」梅林回應著他。

「不對，我穿盔甲保護自己，是因為我要出去打仗。」

「那難道不是為了你害怕會受傷或給殺死嗎？」梅林問。

「人不都怕死嗎？」

梅林搖搖頭：「誰說你一定要去打仗的呢？」

「我要證明，我是個心地好、善良，又充滿了愛的武士。」

「如果你真的是心地好、善良，又充滿了愛，為什麼你還需要去證明呢？」

這個問題讓武士的頭又痛了起來，他用老法子來逃避——去睡覺。

第二天早上，他醒過來，有了個奇怪的想法：可不可能他心地不好、不善良，又沒有充滿了愛？他決定去問梅林。

ask Merlin.

"What do you think?" Merlin replied.

"Why do you always answer a question with another question?"

"And why do you always seek the answers to your questions from others?"

The knight stomped off angrily, cursing Merlin under his breath. "That Merlin!" he muttered. "Sometimes he really gets under my armor!"

With a thud, the knight plunked his burdened body down under a tree to contemplate the magician's questions.

What did he think? "Could it be," he said aloud to no one in particular, "that I'm not good, kind, and loving?"

"Could be," said a little voice. "Otherwise, why are you sitting on my tail?"

"Huh?" The knight peered down to the side and noticed a little squirrel sitting beside him. That is, he could see most of the squirrel. Her tail was hidden from sight.

"Oh, excuse me!" said the knight, quickly moving his leg so that the squirrel could reclaim her tail. "I hope I didn't hurt you. I can't see very well with this visor in my way."

「你説呢？」梅林反過來問他。

「你為什麼老用問題來回答問題？」

「那你為什麼總是要從別人那裡得到問題的答案呢？」

武士氣得直跺腳地走開，小聲地咒罵著法師：「那個梅林，有時候他真讓我受不了。」

帶著笨重的身子，他「砰」的一聲，坐在一棵樹下，思考著法師説的話。

他覺得怎麼樣？「可不可能，」他沒有目的大聲地説：「我心地不好、不善良，也沒有充滿了愛？」

「很可能，」一個小聲音説：「要不然，為什麼你會坐在我的尾巴上？」

「啊？」武士低下頭，看看旁邊，這才發現一隻小松鼠正坐在他的身邊。事實上是，他可以看到松鼠的大部分，可是看不見松鼠的尾巴。

「哦，對不起，」武士説，很快地把腿拿開，讓松鼠可以把尾巴移走。「我希望沒有弄痛妳，我的面盔擋住了視線，我不能看得很清楚。」

"I don't doubt that," replied the squirrel without any resentment in her voice. "That's why you have to keep apologizing to people for hurting them."

"The only thing that irritates me more than a smart-aleck magician is a smart-aleck squirrel," groused the knight. "I don't have to stay here and talk to you."

He labored against the armor's weight in an attempt to get to his feet. Suddenly, in amazement, he blurted out, "Hey... you and I are talking!"

"A tribute to my good nature," replied the squirrel, "considering that you sat on my tail."

"But animals can't talk," said the knight.

"Oh, sure we can," said the squirrel. "It's just that people don't listen."

The knight shook his head in bewilderment. "You've talked to me before?"

"Certainly, every time I cracked a nut and pushed it through your visor."

"How can I hear you now when I couldn't hear you then?"

"I admire an inquiring mind," commented the squirrel, "but don't you ever accept anything the way it is – just because it is?"

"You're answering my questions with questions," said the knight. "You've been around Merlin too long."

「想必如此，」松鼠回答，顯然毫無怨恨：「這就是你一直弄痛別人，不停向人道歉的原因。」

「比自以為是的法師更讓我受不了的，就是自以為是的松鼠。」武士發著牢騷：「我不必待在這裡和妳說話。」

他努力地想讓穿了盔甲的身體站起來，突然，他驚訝地停住：「嘿……我們兩個剛剛在說話。」

「這要歸功於我的性情好，如果我們考慮到你剛剛坐在我尾巴上的話。」松鼠回答道。

「可是動物不會說話。」

「哦，我們當然會說話，」松鼠說：「只是人類不聽罷了。」

武士不可置信地搖著頭：「妳以前和我說過話嗎？」

「當然有，每一次我咬碎核果，推進你面盔裡的時候，我都有說話。」

「為什麼那時候我聽不到，可是現在可以聽見了？」

「我很敬佩你孜孜不倦發問的精神，可是為什麼你不乾脆接受事情的真相？」

「妳用問題回答問題，妳跟梅林在一起太久了。」

"And you haven't been around him long enough!"

The squirrel flicked her tail at the knight and ran up a tree. The knight called after her. "Wait! What's your name?"

"Squirrel," she replied very simply and vanished into the topmost branches.

Dazed, the knight shook his head. Had he imagined all this? At that moment, he saw Merlin approaching. "Merlin," he said, "I have to get out of here. I've started talking to squirrels."

"Splendid." replied the magician.

The knight looked troubled. "What do you mean, splendid?"

"Just that. You are becoming sensitive enough to feel the vibrations of others."

The knight was obviously confused, so Merlin continued explaining. "You did not talk to the squirrel in words, but you felt her vibrations, and you translated those vibrations into words. I am looking forward to the day when you start talking to flowers."

"That'll be the day you plant them on my grave. I have to get out of these woods!"

"Where would you go?"

「而你和他在一起還不夠久。」松鼠用尾巴掃了武士一下，爬上樹去。

武士在後面叫她：「等一等，妳叫什麼名字？」

「松鼠。」她簡單地回答，消失在樹的頂端。

仍然目瞪口呆，武士搖著頭，這是不是他的幻想？就在那時，他看到梅林走了過來。「梅林，」他說：「我得離開這裡，我開始跟松鼠說話了。」

「太好了。」法師回答。

武士看來很困惑：「你是什麼意思？太好了？」

「真的，你現在變得夠敏銳，可以感受到別人的振動。」

武士顯然還是不懂，所以梅林繼續解釋：「你其實並沒有真正和松鼠說話，只是感受到她的振動，然後把振動翻譯成話，我正等著你開始和花朵說話的那一天。」

「那就是你在我墳上種花的那一天。」武士說：「我一定要離開這裡。」

「你要去哪裡？」

"Back to Juliet and Christopher. They've been alone for too long. I have to get back and take care of them."

"How can you take care of them when you cannot even take care of yourself?" Merlin asked.

"But I miss them," whined the knight. "I want to go back to them in the worst way."

"And that is exactly how you will be going back if you go in your armor," cautioned Merlin.

The knight looked at Merlin sadly, "I don't want to wait until I get the armor off. I want to go back now and be a good, kind, and loving husband to Juliet and a great father to Christopher."

Merlin nodded in understanding. He told the knight that going back to give of himself was a lovely gift. "However, a gift, to be a gift, has to be accepted. Otherwise it lies like a burden between people."

"You mean they might not want me back?" asked the knight in surprise. "Surely they would give me another chance. After all, I am one of the top knights in the kingdom."

"Perhaps that armor is thicker than it appears," Merlin said gently.

The knight thought about this. He remembered Juliet's endless

「回到茱莉亞和克斯的身邊，他們已經孤單太久了，我要回家去照顧他們。」

「你還不能照顧自己，怎麼能夠照顧他們？」梅林問他。

「可是我真的好想他們，」武士說：「就算要面對最糟的情況，我也想回家。」

「如果你還穿著盔甲回去的話，那真的就是最糟的情況了。」梅林提醒他。

武士悲傷地看著梅林：「我不想等到脫掉了盔甲再回去，我想現在回去做茱莉亞的好丈夫和克斯的好爸爸。」

梅林了解地點點頭，告訴武士，回去付出自己是件很美的禮物。「可是，」他說：「禮物之所以成為禮物，端看被不被接受，不然，就會變成雙方的負擔。」

「你是說，他們不想要我回家？」武士說，看起來很驚訝：「為什麼？我是全國最優秀的武士。」

「也許你的盔甲比看起來的還厚一點。」梅林溫和地說。

武士想了一想，他想起茱莉亞抱怨他老是在打仗，老是花時間在顧影自憐，還有抱怨他關上面盔，為了要讓她閉嘴，就突

complaints about his going off to battle so often, about the attention he showered on his armor, and about his closed visor and his habit of abruptly going to sleep to shut out her words. Maybe Juliet wouldn't want him back, but certainly Christopher would.

"Why not send Christopher a note and ask him?" suggested Merlin.

The knight agreed that this was a good idea, but how could he get the note to Christopher? Merlin pointed to the pigeon sitting on his shoulder. "Rebecca will take it."

The knight was puzzled. "She doesn't know where I live. She's only a stupid bird."

"I can tell north from south and east from west," snapped Rebecca, "which is more than I can say for you."

The knight quickly apologized. He was thoroughly shaken. Not only had he talked to both a pigeon and a squirrel, but he'd gotten both of them mad at him in the same day.

Bighearted bird that she was, Rebecca accepted the knight's apology and flew off with his hastily written note to Christopher in her beak.

"Don't coo at any strange pigeons, or you'll drop my note," the knight called after her.

然去睡覺的習慣，也許茱莉亞不想要他回去，但是克斯一定會要他回去的。

「為什麼不捎個信給克斯，問問他？」梅林提議。

武士也覺得這是個好主意，可是，他要怎麼才能把信送到克斯手上？梅林指著站在他肩膀上的鴿子：「瑞蓓卡可以送信。」

武士很困惑：「可是她不曉得我住在哪裡，她只是一隻笨鳥罷了。」

「我分得清東南西北，」瑞蓓卡反擊：「光這點就比你強得多。」

武士很快地道了歉，他相當驚嚇，畢竟這是頭一回——在同一天，惹一隻鴿子和一隻松鼠生氣。

不過瑞蓓卡天生寬宏大量，接受了武士的道歉，嘴裡含著武士倉促寫給克斯的紙條，向外飛了出去。

「不要和別的鴿子打情罵俏，不然妳會把紙條丟掉！」武士在後面叫著。

Rebecca ignored his thoughtless remark, realizing that the knight had much to learn.

A week passed, and Rebecca still had not returned. The knight became more and more anxious, fearing she might have fallen prey to one of the hunting falcons he and the other knights had trained. He winced, wondering how he could have participated in such a foul sport – then winced again at his awful pun.

When Merlin finished playing his lute and singing "You'll Have a Long, Cold Winter if You Have a Short, Cold Heart," the knight expressed his worries about Rebecca.

Merlin reassured the knight by making up a happy little verse:

"The smartest pigeon who ever flew

will never wind up in someone's stew."

All at once, a great chattering arose from the animals. They were all looking skyward, so Merlin and the knight looked, too. High above them, circling for a landing, they saw Rebecca.

The knight struggled to his feet just as Rebecca swooped down onto Merlin's shoulder. Taking the note from her beak, the magician glanced at it and gravely told the knight that it was from Christopher.

瑞蓓卡對這種欠考慮的話置之不理，她知道武士還有很多需要學習的地方。

　　一個星期過去了，瑞蓓卡仍然沒有回來。武士越來越焦慮，害怕她可能變成被其他武士訓練出來的獵鷹的獵物。他搖搖頭，奇怪自己以前怎麼能參加這麼「鳥」的打鳥遊戲，這個雙關語又讓他苦笑了一聲。

　　等梅林邊彈邊唱完那首〈汝有窄冷心，必有長寒冬〉，武士告訴梅林他正在害怕的事。

　　梅林說，他不怕鴿子會變成別人的盤中飧，說著說著，他即席創作了兩句快樂短詩，他唱著：

　　「任邀翔之聰明鴿，

　　會自保不受宰割。」

　　突然，一陣鳥鳴聲驚動了所有的動物，大家往天空望去，沒錯，在那裡盤旋著要降落的就是瑞蓓卡。

　　武士掙扎著站起來，瑞蓓卡落在梅林的肩上，梅林把紙條從她的嘴裡取下來，看了一眼，嚴肅地告訴武士，那是克斯的回信。

"Let me see!" said the knight, eagerly seizing the paper. His jaw dropped with a clank as he stared at the note in disbelief. "It's blank!" he exclaimed. "What does that mean?"

"It means," said Merlin softly, "that your son does not know enough about you to give you an answer."

The knight stood there for a moment, stunned, then groaned and slowly sank to the ground. He tried to choke back the tears, for knights in shining armor simply didn't cry. However, his grief soon overwhelmed him. Then, exhausted and half-drowned from the tears in his helmet, the knight fell asleep.

「讓我看。」武士説，著急地抓住那張信紙，他不可置信地看著信，下巴驚訝地掉了下來，「是張白紙！」他大叫：「這是什麼意思？」

　　「這是説，」梅林溫和地説：「你兒子對你的了解不夠，不能回答你的問題。」

　　武士愣在當場，説不出話來。他呻吟著、慢慢地，又帶點噭嘎聲地倒在地上。他試著想忍住眼淚，因為穿著閃亮盔甲的武士是不哭的，可是他的悲傷淹沒了一切。然後，哭累了，又差點給留在頭盔裡的淚水淹死，武士終於睡著了。

真理之道

The Path of Truth

The Path of Truth

When the knight awoke. Merlin was sitting quietly beside him.

"I'm sorry I acted so unknightly," said the knight. "My beard got all soggy," he added in disgust.

"Do not apologize," said Merlin. "You have just taken the first step toward getting out of your armor."

"What do you mean?"

"You will see," replied the magician. He stood up. "It is time for you to go."

This disturbed the knight. He had come to enjoy staying in the woods with Merlin and the animals. Anyway it seemed he had no place to go. Juliet and Christopher apparently didn't want him to come home. True, he could get back into the knight business and go on some crusades. He had a good reputation in battle, and there were several kings who would be happy to have him, but fighting no longer seemed to have any purpose.

Merlin reminded the knight of his new purpose: to get rid of his armor.

真理之道

　　武士醒過來的時候，發現梅林靜靜地坐在他身邊。

　　「對不起，我表現得一點也不像個武士，」說著，又厭惡地加上一句：「我的鬍子都濕透了。」

　　「別說抱歉，」梅林說：「你剛剛做了脫離盔甲的第一步。」

　　「這是什麼意思？」

　　「你會明白的，」法師回答，他站了起來，「你應該上路了。」

　　武士有點不安，他開始喜歡和梅林，和其他動物一起待在樹林裡。而且，現在他也沒有別的地方可去，顯然茱莉亞和克斯也不想要他回家。沒錯，他是可以回去再幹武士這一行，他的作戰紀錄很好，不少國王會很樂意收留他。可是為什麼要打仗呢？似乎沒有什麼意義了。

　　梅林提醒他，新的目標是把盔甲丟掉。

"Why bother?" asked the knight morosely. "It doesn't matter to Juliet and Christopher whether I get my armor off or not."

"Do it for yourself," suggested Merlin. "Being trapped in all that steel has caused you a lot of problems, and things will only get worse as time goes on. You could even die of something like catching pneumonia from a soggy beard."

"I suppose my armor has become a nuisance," replied the knight. "I'm tired of lugging it around, and I'm fed up with eating mushy food. Come to think of it, I can't even scratch my back when it itches."

"And how long has it been since you have felt the warmth of a kiss, smelled the fragrance of a flower, or heard a beautiful melody without your armor getting in the way?"

"I can hardly remember," mumbled the knight sadly. "You're right, Merlin. I have to get this armor off for myself."

"You cannot continue living and thinking as you have in the past," said Merlin. "That is how you got stuck in your steel prison in the first place."

"But how am I ever going to change all that?" asked the knight uneasily.

"It is not as difficult as it may seem," Merlin explained, leading the knight to a path. "This was the path you followed to get into these woods."

「有什麼用呢？」武士垂頭喪氣地說：「茱莉亞和克斯根本不關心我能不能把盔甲脫下來。」

「你要為自己把盔甲脫下來，」梅林說：「困在這件鐵甲裡已經給你造成許多困擾，而且繼續下去情況會變得更糟，你可能會因為弄濕鬍子而感染肺炎這種事，送掉一條命。」

「我想我的盔甲已經變成一個大累贅了，」武士回答：「成天拖著這麼件東西，只能吃黏糊糊的食物實在很煩，想想看，我連背癢的時候都抓不到。」

「因為有這件盔甲擋著，有多久，你沒有感受過一個吻的暖意、一朵花的香味，或是聽見一首優美旋律的曲子了？」

「太久了，我都不記得了，」武士悲傷地小聲說著：「你是對的，梅林，我一定要為自己把這件盔甲脫掉。」

梅林說：「你不能再像以前那樣的生活和思考，因為那就是你給卡在這一堆廢鐵裡的原因。」

「但是我要怎麼樣才能改變現狀呢？」武士不安地問。

「事情不像看起來那麼困難，」梅林一邊解釋，一邊領著武士走到一條小路前：「你就是走這條路才進了樹林的。」

"I didn't follow any path," said the knight. "I was lost for months!"

"People are often unaware of the path they are on," replied Merlin.

"You mean this path was here, but I couldn't see it?"

"Yes, and you can go back that way if you want, but it leads to dishonesty, greed, hatred, jealousy, fear, and ignorance."

"Are you spying that I am all those things?" the knight asked indignantly.

"At times, you are some of those things," Merlin admitted quietly.

The magician then pointed to another path. It was narrower than the first and very steep.

"That looks like a tough climb," observed the knight.

Merlin nodded in agreement. "That," he said, "is the Path of Truth. It gets steeper as it approaches the summit of a mountain far in the distance."

The knight looked at the steep trail without enthusiasm. "I'm not sure it's worth it. What will I have when I get to the top?"

"It is what you won't have," Merlin explained– "your armor!" The knight pondered this. If he returned to the path that he had traveled before, there was no hope of removing his armor, and he would probably die of loneliness and fatigue. The only way to get the armor off, it seemed, was to follow the Path of Truth, but then he might die trying to struggle up the steep

「我並沒沿著什麼路，」武士說：「我迷路了好幾個月！」

「人們通常不能意識到自己走在什麼路上。」梅林答。

「你的意思是說，這條路一直在這裡，只是我看不見？」

「對，你也可以從這條路回家，這條路通向虛偽、貪婪、仇恨、嫉妒、恐懼，和無知。」

「你是說，這些缺點我都有嗎？」武士生氣地問。

「有時候，你每一樣都有一點。」梅林輕聲地回應。

然後法師指著另一條路，那一條路比第一條路狹窄，而且非常陡峭。

「那條路看來有得爬了。」武士觀察著。

梅林同意地點著頭，說：「那就是真理之道，越往遠方的山頂就越陡。」

武士毫不起勁地望著那條陡路：「走這條路到底值不值得？到了山頂，我能得到什麼？」

「你能丟掉不要的東西──你的盔甲。」梅林說。

武士想了一想，如果他由原路回去，脫掉盔甲絕對沒希望，也很可能會被寂寞和疲倦給壓死。看來脫掉盔甲的唯一一條路就是走上真理之道，可是話又說回來，他也可能在努力往上爬

mountainside.

The knight looked at the difficult path ahead. Then he looked down at the steel covering his body.

"OK," he said with resignation. "I'll try the Path of Truth."

Merlin nodded. "Your decision to take an unknown trail while encumbered with heavy armor takes great courage."

The knight knew that he'd better start immediately, or he might change his mind. "I'll get my trusty horse," he said.

"Oh, no," said Merlin, shaking his head. "The path has areas too narrow for a horse to pass. You will have to go on foot."

Aghast, the knight plunked down on a rock. "I think I'd rather die of a soggy beard," he said, his courage waning rapidly.

"You will not have to travel alone," Merlin told him. "Squirrel will accompany you."

"What do you expect me to do, ride squirrel-back?" asked the knight, dreading the thought of making the arduous journey with a smart-talking animal.

"You might not be able to ride me," said Squirrel, "but you'll need me to help you eat. Who else is going to chew nuts for you and push them through

的半路上累死。

武士看著眼前的這條陡路，再低頭看看包裹在身上的鐵衣。

「好吧，」他下定決心的說：「我要試試真理之道。」

梅林點點頭：「帶著這麼重的盔甲走上未知之路，這個決定需要很大的勇氣。」

武士知道自己最好在改變主意以前，馬上上路。「我去牽馬。」他說。

「哦，不行，」梅林搖著頭說：「這條路太窄，馬過不去，你得步行。」

武士嚇得像洩了氣的氣球一樣坐在石頭上。「那麼我寧可因鬍子濕了感冒而死。」

「你不必一個人走，」梅林告訴他：「松鼠可以陪你去。」

「你希望我怎麼辦？騎松鼠嗎？」武士說。他害怕和一隻能言善道的動物走這麼難走的路。

「也許你不能騎我，」松鼠說：「可是你需要我餵你，誰還能把堅果咬爛，推進你的面盔裡給你吃？」

your visor?"

Rebecca flew over from a nearby tree, where she'd heard the conversation, and landed on the knight's shoulder. "I'll go with you, too. I've been to the top of the mountain, and I know the way," she said.

The willingness of the two animals to help gave the knight the courage he needed.

Well, isn't this something, he said to himself, one of the top knights in the kingdom needing courage from a squirrel and a bird! He struggled to his feet, signaling to Merlin that he was ready to begin his journey.

As they walked toward the path, the magician took an exquisite golden key from his neck and gave it to the knight. "This key will open the doors to three castles that will block your path."

"I know!" cried the knight eagerly. "There will be a princess inside each castle, and I'll slay the dragon guarding her and rescue …"

"Enough!" Merlin broke in. "There will be no princesses in any of these castles. Even if there were, you are in no shape just now to be rescuing anyone. You have to learn to save yourself first."

Thus reprimanded, the knight grew quiet while Merlin continued. "The first castle is named Silence; the second, Knowledge; and the third, Will

聽到他們的談話，瑞蓓卡從附近一棵樹飛過來，停在武士的肩上，說：「我跟你們一起去，我到過山頂，我知道路怎麼走。」

這兩隻動物的自願幫忙給了武士所需要的額外勇氣。

他跟自己說，這真有意思，全國最頂尖之一的武士需要一隻松鼠和一隻鳥來加油！他掙扎地站了起來，向梅林表示他準備啟程。

法師從脖子上取下一把精緻的金鑰匙，在他們朝那條路走過去的時候，把鑰匙交給了武士。「這把鑰匙可以打開擋在路中間三座城堡的大門。」

「我知道！」武士大聲地說：「每一座城堡裡有一個公主，我會殺死看守她的惡龍，然後拯救……」

「夠了！別說這些童話了。」梅林打斷他：「城堡裡沒有公主，更何況，你現在的狀況也不適合去救公主，你得要先拯救自己才行。」

給這麼罵了一頓，武士閉上嘴，聽梅林往下說：「第一座城堡叫沉默之堡，第二座叫知識之堡，第三座，志勇之堡。一旦

and Daring. Once you enter them, you will find your way out only after you have learned what you are there to learn."

From the knight's point of view, this didn't sound like nearly as much fun as rescuing princesses. Besides, at the moment, castle tours didn't really appeal to him. "Why can't I just go around the castles?" he asked sulkily.

"If you do, you'll stray from the path, and you are certain to get lost. The only way you can get to the top of the mountain is to go through those castles," Merlin said firmly.

The knight sighed deeply as he gazed up the steep, narrow trail. It disappeared between tall trees that jutted up toward some low-hanging clouds. He sensed that this journey was going to be much more difficult than a crusade.

Merlin knew what the knight was thinking. "Yes," he agreed, "there is a different battle to be fought on the Path of Truth. The fight will be learning to love yourself."

"How will I do that?" asked the knight.

"It will begin with learning to know yourself," answered Merlin. "This battle cannot be won with your sword, so you can leave it here." Merlin's gentle gaze rested on the knight for a moment. Then he added, "If you

進入城堡，要等到學會該學習的東西之後，你才能找到出去的路。」

對武士而言，這一點也不像拯救公主那麼好玩，更何況，武士目前對城堡之旅毫無興趣。「為什麼我不繞過去就算了？」他悶悶不樂地問。

「如果繞過城堡，你就會遠離正道，然後迷路。到山頂的唯一一條路，就是穿過這些城堡。」梅林堅定地說。

武士望著陡峭、狹窄的路嘆著氣，那條路在高聳入靄靄白雲的大樹中消失，他感覺到這趟旅行會比打聖戰還要艱難得多。

梅林知道他在想什麼。「對，」他同意：「在真理之道上打的仗是不一樣的——這場仗就是學習如何愛自己。」

「我該怎麼做呢？」武士問。

「從學習認識自己開始。」梅林回答。「帶著劍是打不贏的，所以你把劍留下來。」梅林溫和的眼光在武士的身上停留了一下，然後他加了一句：「如果你碰到不能處理的事，只要呼喚我，我就會出現。」

encounter anything you cannot handle, just call me, and I will come."

"You mean you can appear anywhere I happen to be?"

"Any self-respecting magician can do that," Merlin replied. Then he disappeared.

The knight was astounded. "Why...why, he vanished!"

Squirrel nodded. "He really hams it up sometimes."

"You're going to waste all your energy talking," Rebecca scolded. "Let's get going."

The knight's helmet squeaked as he shook his head in assent. They started out with Squirrel in the lead, then the knight with Rebecca on his shoulder. From time to time, Rebecca flew on scouting missions and returned to report what lay ahead.

After a few hours, the knight collapsed, exhausted and sore. He was not used to traveling in armor without his horse. Since it was almost dark anyway, Rebecca and Squirrel decided that they might as well stop there for the night.

Rebecca flew among the bushes and returned with some berries, which she pushed through the holes in the knight's visor. Squirrel went to a nearby brook and filled some walnut shells with water, which the knight drank through the straw that Merlin had given him. Too tired to stay awake for the

「你是說，你能隨心所欲地現身？」

「任何自重的法師都可以做得到這點。」梅林回答，邊說邊消失不見。

武士嚇了一跳：「天啊！他消失了。」

松鼠點著頭：「有時候他實在表演得滿過火的。」

「一直說話會浪費你的力氣，」瑞蓓卡罵他：「咱們上路吧！」

武士軋軋作響地點著頭表示同意。他們就這樣上了路：松鼠帶頭，武士殿後，瑞蓓卡坐在武士的肩上。瑞蓓卡三不五時地飛出去觀察地形，再回來報告前面的情況。

過了幾個小時，武士終於崩潰，他又累又痛。他不習慣不騎馬穿盔甲旅行。既然天色將暗，瑞蓓卡和松鼠決定，他們不如就在此休息過夜。

瑞蓓卡在樹叢裡，邊飛邊撿著莓子，回來把莓子塞進武士的面盔裡，松鼠到附近的小溪，用半個胡桃殼裝了水，帶回來給武士，武士再用梅林給的吸管喝水。不過，他累得沒辦法撐到享受松鼠接下來給他收集的堅果。很快的，他就睡著了。

nuts Squirrel was preparing next, the knight fell asleep.

He was awakened the next morning by the sun shining in his eyes. Unaccustomed to the glare, he squinted. His visor had never before allowed in so much light. As he was trying to figure out this phenomenon, he became aware that Squirrel and Rebecca were looking at him, excitedly chattering and cooing. Pushing himself to a sitting position, he suddenly realized that he could see more than he had the day before, and he could feel the cool air against his face. Part of his visor had broken off and fallen away!

How did that happen? he wondered.

Squirrel answered his unspoken question. "It rusted and fell off."

"But how?" asked the knight.

"From the tears you cried after you saw your son's blank letter," said Rebecca.

The knight considered this. The sorrow he had felt was so deep that his armor could not protect him from it. Quite to the contrary, his tears had started to break down the steel surrounding him.

"That's it!" he shouted. "Tears from real feelings will release me from my armor!"

He climbed to his feet faster than he had done in years. "Squirrel!

第二天早晨，武士給照進眼睛的陽光給亮醒。不習慣這麼刺眼的陽光，他眨著眼睛，他的面盔從來不能讓這麼強的陽光照進來。在試著思考其中的緣故時，他發現松鼠和瑞蓓卡在看他，還一邊吱吱喳喳地聊天。武士勉強自己坐起來，突然發現視野變廣了，他可以感覺到輕拂在臉上清涼的空氣。他的面盔有些地方裂開，掉了下來。

　　「這是怎麼回事？」他問自己。

　　松鼠回答了他沒有說出口的問題：「盔甲鏽了，掉了下來。」

　　「這怎麼可能？」武士問。

　　「你看了你兒子空白信之後，哭的眼淚讓盔甲生鏽了。」瑞蓓卡說。

　　武士想了想，他那時的悲傷太強烈，沒有盔甲能保護他，相反的，悲傷的眼淚，開始使包圍他的鐵皮裂開。

　　「這就對了！」他大叫：「真正有感覺的眼淚，可以讓我脫離盔甲！」

　　他用好多年沒有過的快速度站了起來。「松鼠，瑞蓓卡，」他叫著：「騎驢看唱本走著瞧，讓咱們上真理之道。」

Rebecca!" he cried. "Forsooth! Let's hit the Path of Truth!"

Rebecca and Squirrel were so overjoyed at what was happening to the knight that neither of them even mentioned that this was terrible rhyming.

The three of them continued on up the mountain. It was an especially fine day for the knight. He noticed tiny sunlit particles in the air as they filtered through the branches of the trees. He looked closely at the faces of some robins and saw that they didn't all look alike.

He mentioned this to Rebecca who hopped up and down, cooing merrily. "You're starting to see the differences in other forms of life because you're starting to see the differences within yourself."

The knight tried to figure out exactly what Rebecca meant. He was too proud to ask, for he still thought a knight should be smarter than a pigeon.

Just then Squirrel, who had gone scouting ahead, came scampering back. "The Castle of Silence is just over the next rise."

Excited at the thought of seeing the castle, the knight clanked forward even faster. He reached the top of the hill quite out of breath. Sure enough, a castle loomed ahead, completely blocking the path. The knight confessed to Squirrel and Rebecca that he was disappointed. He had expected a very fancy structure. Instead, the Castle of Silence looked just like any other tract castle.

瑞蓓卡和松鼠太為發生的事高興了，沒有人跟武士說，他這兩句話押韻押得真差。

他們三個於是繼續往山上爬。對武士來說，這是個特別美好的一天，他注意到陽光篩過樹枝的小亮點，他仔細地觀察了幾隻知更鳥，發現這些鳥長得不完全一模一樣。

他跟瑞蓓卡提起這件事，瑞蓓卡高興地跳上跳下。「你開始能夠看到生命不同的形式，是因為你開始看到自己內心的不同處。」她咕咕地說。

武士想了一下，試著去推敲瑞蓓卡真正的意思為何。他還是太驕傲，不好意思發問，他總覺得武士應該比鴿子聰明。

就在那時候，出去巡邏的松鼠匆匆忙忙地跑回來。「沉默之堡就在下一個上坡的地方。」她說。

很高興能看到城堡，武士嘰嘰軋軋地走得更快，上氣不接下氣地到了山頂，他向遠方望了過去，一點也沒錯，沉默之堡在前面隱約可見，擋住了去路。武士向松鼠和瑞蓓卡承認，他有一點點失望——他本來以為沉默之堡會更壯觀一點，沒想到，沉默之堡看來就和其他觀光宣傳小冊上的城堡沒什麼兩樣。

Rebecca laughed and said, "When you learn to accept instead of expect, you'll have fewer disappointments."

The knight nodded at the wisdom of this. "I've spent most of my life being disappointed. I remember lying in my crib, thinking I was the most beautiful baby in the whole world. Then my nurse looked down at me and said, 'You have a face only a mother could love.' I wound up being disappointed in myself for being ugly instead of beautiful, and I was disappointed in the nurse for being so impolite."

"If you had truly accepted yourself as beautiful, it wouldn't have mattered what she said. You wouldn't have been disappointed," Squirrel explained.

This made sense to the knight. "I'm beginning to think that animals are smarter than people."

"The fact that you can say that makes you as smart as we are," Squirrel replied.

"I don't think it has anything to do with being smart," said Rebecca. "Animals accept and humans expect. You'll never hear a rabbit say, 'I expect the sun to come out this morning so I can go down to the lake and play.' If the sun doesn't come out, it won't ruin the rabbit's whole day. He's happy just

瑞蓓卡笑著説：「當你學會了接受而不期待，失望就會少得多。」

武士為這句話的智慧點點頭：「我這一生中大部分的時間都在失望，我記得我躺在嬰兒床上，認為自己是全世界最漂亮的小孩。然後保姆低下頭來，看著我説：『只有生你的媽媽才會喜歡你的臉。』結果我對自己長得醜失望，又對她的不禮貌失望。」

松鼠説：「如果你真的認為自己漂亮，她説什麼都無關緊要，你也不會失望。」

對武士來説，這句話大有學問。「我開始覺得動物比人聰明了。」

「你能這樣説，就表示你和我們一樣聰明。」松鼠回答。

「我不認為這和聰明有關係，」瑞蓓卡説：「動物接受，人類期待。你從來不會聽見一隻兔子説：『我希望今早太陽會出來，我好去湖裡玩。』如果太陽沒出來，也不會破壞兔子的一天，光做兔子，兔子就很高興了。」

武士仔細地思考這席話，可是他無法想像，有多少人光是

being a rabbit."

The knight mulled this over. He couldn't recall many people who were happy just being people.

Soon they came to the door of the huge castle. The knight took the golden key from his neck and fitted it into the lock. As he opened the door, Rebecca whispered, "We're not going in with you."

The knight, who was learning to love and trust the two animals, was disappointed that they would not accompany him. He almost said so, but he caught himself. He was expecting again.

The animals knew that the knight was hesitant to step into the castle. "We can show you the door," said Squirrel, "but you have to walk through it alone."

As Rebecca flew off, she called cheerily, "We'll meet you on the other side."

做人就會開心的。

很快的，他們到達城堡的大門前，武士掏出梅林給他的金鑰匙，插進了匙孔裡，他轉動鑰匙開門的時候，瑞蓓卡說：「我們不跟你進去。」

武士剛學會了怎麼去愛和信任這兩隻動物，因此很失望他們不能陪他進去。他差點把想法說出來，然而還是忍住，他又在期待了。

兩隻動物知道他有點怕走進一座毫無所知的城堡裡。「我們只能告訴你門在哪裡，」松鼠說：「可是，你需要自己一個人穿過那些門。」

瑞蓓卡在飛走的時候叫著：「我們在城堡的那一頭等你。」

沉默之堡

The Castle of Silence

The Castle of Silence

Left on his own, the knight cautiously poked his head inside the doorway of the castle. His knees trembled slightly, which, with his armor, caused him to make a low metallic rattle. Not wanting to look chicken to a pigeon in case Rebecca could still see him, he pulled himself together and walked boldly inside, closing the door after him.

For a moment, he wished he hadn't left his sword behind, but Merlin had promised that there,d be no dragons to slay, and the knight trusted him.

He walked into the huge anteroom of the castle and he looked around. He saw only a fire blazing in an enormous stone fireplace on one wall and three rugs on the floor. He sat down on the rug nearest the fire.

The knight soon became aware of two things: First, there seemed to be no door leading out of the room to other parts of the castle. Second, there was an extraordinary, eerie silence in this castle. He realized with a start that the fire wasn't even crackling. The knight had thought of his own castle as quiet, especially at those times when Juliet didn't talk to him for several days,

沉默之堡

匹馬單槍一個人，武士小心地把頭伸進城堡的大門裡，他的膝蓋有點顫抖，發出一響聲。不過不想讓一隻鴿子看到他的「鳥」相，他振作了一下，勇敢地走進大門，把門關上。

一走進城堡，他就後悔當初沒把劍帶來。然而，梅林保證過城堡裡無龍可屠，武士相信他。

他走進堡內寬闊的前廳，四處張望著。除了三張地毯之外，廳裡沒有其他的傢俱。他坐在大壁爐前的地毯上，爐裡的火熊熊地燃燒著。

很快的，他發現兩件事：第一，這個房間看起來好像沒有門通到堡裡其他的地方；第二，房間裡有股古怪的、全然的寂靜。他吃驚地發現連壁爐裡的火都沒有發出劈哩叭啦的聲響。他以前認為自己的城堡算是安靜的了，特別是茱莉亞跟他冷戰好幾天的時候，可是那種安靜和這裡的不一樣。沉默之堡真是名副其

but it was nothing like this. The Castle of Silence is well named, he thought. Never in his life had he felt so alone.

Suddenly, the knight was startled by the sound of a familiar voice behind him.

"Hello, Knight."

The knight turned and was astonished to see the king approaching him from a far corner of the room.

"King!" he gasped. "I didn't even see you. What are you doing here?"

"The same thing you are. Knight – looking for the door."

The knight looked around again. "I don't see any door."

"One can't really see until one understands," said the king. "When you understand what's in this room, you'll be able to see the door to the next."

"I certainly hope so. King," said the knight. "I'm surprised to see you here. I heard you were on a crusade."

"That's the word I give out whenever I travel the Path of Truth," the king explained. "It's easier for my subjects to understand."

The knight looked puzzled.

"Everybody understands crusades," said the king, "but very few understand truth."

實，他從來沒有覺得這麼孤單過。

突然，身後響起了一個熟悉的聲音，武士嚇了一大跳。

「哈囉，武士。」

武士轉過身，很震驚地看到國王從房間的另一角向他走過來。

「陛下，」他吸了一口氣：「我剛才根本沒看到你，你在這裡做什麼？」

「和你一樣，武士，找門出去。」

武士四處望望，很困惑：「我沒看到有什麼門。」

「人要在了解以後，才能真正的看見，」國王說：「等你了解到這個房間裡有什麼的時候，你就可以看到通往下一個房間的門了。」

「但願如此，陛下。」武士說：「我真的很意外在這裡看到你，我聽說你去參加聖戰了。」

國王解釋道：「那是官方發布的說法，每當我到真理之道來尋求真理的時候，那種說法比較容易懂。」

武士看來一頭霧水。

「人人都知道聖戰是什麼，」國王說：「可是很少人了解

"Yes," agreed the knight. "I wouldn't be on this path myself if I weren't trapped in this armor."

"Most of us are trapped inside our armor," declared the king.

"What do you mean?" asked the knight.

"We set up barriers to protect who we think we are. Then one day we get stuck behind the barriers, and we can't get out."

"I never thought of you as being stuck. King. You're so wise," said the knight.

The king laughed ruefully. "I have enough wisdom to know when I'm stuck and to return here so that I can learn more about myself."

The knight was greatly encouraged, thinking that perhaps the king could show him the way. "Say," said the knight, his face brightening, "could we go through the castle together? That way we wouldn't be so lonely."

The king shook his head. "I once tried that. It's true that my companions and I weren't lonely because we talked constantly, but when one talks, it's impossible to see the door out of this room."

"Maybe we could just walk along and be quiet together," suggested the knight. He wasn't looking forward to wandering around the Castle of Silence by himself.

真理。」

「對，」武士同意地點點頭：「如果我不是給困在這身盔甲裡的話，我也不會踏上這條路。」

「大多數的人都穿了一身的盔甲。」國王強調。

「你是什麼意思？」武士問。

「我們設下障礙來保護我們自己所謂的自我。然後有一天，我們就給關在這些障礙裡面，無法掙脫。」

「我從來沒想過你也會給困住，陛下。」武士說：「你是那麼有智慧。」

國王悲傷地笑著：「對，我是有足夠智慧，可以告訴自己什麼時候被困住，所以我能再回來這裡，學習更了解自己。」

武士覺得受到很大的鼓勵，想著國王也許可以指點他一條明路。「我說，」武士說著，臉發亮了起來：「我們可不可以一起通過城堡？這樣我們就不會覺得太孤單。」

國王搖搖頭：「有一次我試過，這樣一來，我和我的同伴的確都不會覺得孤單，因為我們一直在說話。可是只要有人說話，我們就看不到離開房間的門在哪裡。」

「也許我們可以只是一塊走，不說話。」武士說。他可不

The king shook his head again, harder this time. "No, I tried that, too. It made the emptiness less painful, but I still couldn't see the door out of this room."

The knight protested. "But if you weren't talking..."

"Being quiet is more than not talking," said the king. "I discovered that when I was with someone, I showed only my best image. I wouldn't let down my barriers and allow either myself or the other person to see what I was trying to hide."

"I don't get it," said the knight.

"You will," replied the king, "when you have been here long enough. One must be alone to drop one's armor."

The knight was dismayed. "I don't want to stay here by myself!" he exclaimed, stamping his foot emphatically and inadvertently bringing it down on the king's big toe.

The king yelled in pain and hopped around.

The knight was horrified! First the smith; now the king. "Sorry, sire," said the knight apologetically.

The king rubbed his toe tenderly. "Oh, well. That armor hurts you more than it hurts me." Then, standing tall, he looked knowingly at the knight. "I

想一個人在沉默之堡裡四處遊盪。

國王搖搖頭，這次更用力了點：「我也試過那麼做，那樣會讓寂寞感不那麼可怕，不過我還是找不到離開房間的門。」

武士抗議：「可是如果不說話……」

「沉默不只是不說話而已，」國王回答：「我發現只要和別人在一起，我就只會把最好的一面呈現出來，不能把障礙放下，讓自己或是別人看看想要隱藏的是什麼。」

「我不懂。」武士說。

「你會懂的，」國王回答：「等你在這裡待得夠久的時候。人要獨處，才能脫掉自己的盔甲。」

武士看來很驚慌。「我不要一個人待在這裡！」他大叫，強調重點似地用力跺著腳，一不小心踩到國王的大腳趾。國王痛苦地尖叫起來，抱著腳四處跳著。

武士嚇壞了，先是鐵匠，現在又是國王。「對不起，陛下。」武士抱歉地說。

國王輕輕地揉著他的腳趾。「哦，沒關係，你的盔甲給你帶來的痛苦，比你給我的痛苦多得多。」他站直了身體，了解地

understand that you don't want to stay in this castle by yourself. Neither did I when I first began coming here, but now I realize that what one must do here, one must do alone." With that, he limped across the room, adding, "I must be on my way now."

Perplexed, the knight asked, "Where are you going? The door is over here."

"That door is only an entrance. The door to the next room is on the far wall. I finally saw it just as you came in," said the king.

"What do you mean you finally saw it? Didn't you remember where it was from the other times you were here?" asked the knight, wondering why the king would bother to keep coming back.

"One never finishes traveling the Path of Truth. Each time I come here, I find new doors as I understand more and more." The king waved. "Be good to yourself, my friend."

"Wait! Please!" called the knight.

The king looked back at him compassionately. "Yes?"

The knight knew well that he couldn't shake the king's resolve. "Is there any advice you can give me before you go?"

The king thought for a moment then replied, "This is a new kind of

看著武士：「我知道你不想一個人待在這座城堡裡，我第一次來的時候也不想，但是我現在了解到，在這裡要完成的事，一定得一個人自己完成。」跛著腳穿過房間的時候，國王加上一句：「我得繼續上路了。」

武士迷惑地問：「你要去哪裡？門在這裡。」

「那扇門是入口，」國王解釋：「通往另一個房間的門在那邊的牆上，你進來的時候我才終於看到。」

「你說你終於看到門是什麼意思？你以前來的時候不記得門在哪裡嗎？」武士問，他不懂國王為什麼老要回到這座城堡。

「真理之道的路是走不完的，每次我來的時候，了解得越多，就會找到更多新的門。」國王揮揮手：「好好照顧自己，我的朋友。」

「等一下，拜託。」武士叫著。

國王回頭看他，同情地應著：「什麼事情？」

武士很清楚他沒辦法動搖國王的決心：「走之前，你能不能給我一些建議？」

國王想了想，然後回答：「對你而言，這是場嶄新的聖

crusade for you, dear Knight – one that requires more courage than all the other battles you've known before. It will be your greatest victory if you can summon the strength to stay and do what you need to do here."

With this, the king turned, reached out as if to open a door, then disappeared into the wall, leaving the knight staring disbelievingly after him.

The knight hurried over to where the king had been, hoping that from up close, he might be able to see the door, too. Finding what appeared to be only a solid wall, he began to pace around the room. All the knight could hear was the sound of his armor echoing through the castle.

After awhile, he felt more depressed than ever in his life. To cheer himself up, he sang a couple of rousing battle songs: "I'll Be Down to Get You in a Crusade, Honey" and "Anywhere I Hang My Helmet is Home." He sang them over and over again.

As his voice grew tired, the stillness began to drown out his singing, enveloping him in utter, devastating quiet. Only then could the knight frankly admit something he'd never acknowledged before: He was afraid to be alone.

At that moment, he saw a door in the far wall of the room. He crossed over to it, slowly pulled it open, and stepped into another room. This chamber appeared very much like the last, except it was somewhat smaller. It,

戰──打這場聖戰需要的勇氣，比你以前打所有的仗加起來所需要的勇氣還要多。如果你能鼓起勇氣留下來，做你該做的事，這會是你這一生中最大的勝利。」

說完，國王轉過身，伸出手彷彿在開門，然後就在牆中間消失，留下武士在身後不可置信地瞪大眼望著。

武士連忙跑到國王消失的地方，希望靠近一點能讓他看到門在哪裡，但是眼前只有一堵堅實的牆。他開始在房間裡走來走去，聽到的聲音只有自己盔甲碰撞的回響。

過了一會兒，他開始感受到一輩子也沒有經驗過的沮喪。為了讓自己開心一點，他開始唱起振奮人心的戰歌〈甜心，我將為妳上戰場〉，還有〈繫頭盔處即是兒家〉。他一遍又一遍地唱著。

慢慢的，他的聲音累了，寂靜開始淹沒他的歌聲，全然、具毀滅性的寂靜重重地將他包圍起來。到那個時候，武士終於承認了一件他從來沒有發現過的事──他害怕獨處。

就在那時，他看見房間另一邊的牆上出現一扇門。越過房間，他小心地打開門，走進另一間房間裡。這間房間和前一間很

too, was void of all sound.

In order to pass the time, the knight began talking aloud to himself. He said anything that came into his mind. He talked about what he was like as a little boy and how he was different from the other boys he knew. While they hunted quail and played "Pin the Tail on the Boar," he sat inside and read. Since books were handwritten by the monks then, they were few, and he had soon read them all. That is when he began talking eagerly to anyone who passed his way. When there was no one to talk to, he talked to himself – just as he was doing now. He unexpectedly found himself saying that he had talked so much all his life to keep himself from feeling alone.

The knight thought hard about this until the sound of his own voice broke the chilling silence. "I guess I've always been afraid to be alone."

As he spoke these words, another door became visible. The knight opened it and stepped into the next room. It was smaller than the previous one.

He sat on the floor and continued thinking. Soon the thought struck him that all his life he had wasted time talking about what he had done and what he was going to do. He'd never enjoyed what was happening at the time. And yet another door appeared. It led to a room still smaller than the others.

相似，只是好像小一點，但也同樣寂靜無聲。

　　武士開始大聲自言自語來打發時間，講任何他想到的事。他談到自己小時候是什麼樣子，怎麼和其他認識的小孩不同，其他的小孩打鵪鶉，唱〈把尾巴釘在野豬身上〉，他卻在房裡讀書。不過因為那時候大部分的書都是僧侶手寫的，所以能讀的書不多，很快他就讀完了所有的書。之後他就開始熱切地和任何遇到的人說話，沒有人說話的時候，他就和自己說，就像他現在在做的一樣。說著說著，發現自己竟說道：他這生之所以會這麼喜歡說話的原因，就是為了不讓自己覺得孤單。

　　武士認真思考著這個想法，直到自己的聲音劃破凜冽的沉寂：「我想其實我一直都很害怕獨處。」

　　說完這句話以後，另一扇門馬上在牆上顯現出來。武士打開門。走進下一間房間，這間房間比前一間更小。

　　他坐在地板上開始想，突然醒悟，他這一輩子的時間不是浪費在高談闊論過去的功績；就是在誇耀自己未來的計畫，卻從沒有享受過當下發生的事。然後，另一扇門在牆上出現，通向比前三間更小的房間。

Encouraged by his progress, the knight did something he'd never done before. He sat still and listened to the silence. It occurred to him that for most of his life, he hadn't really listened to anyone or anything. The rustle of the wind, the patter of the rain, and the sound of water running through the brooks must have always been there, but he never actually heard them. Nor had he heard Juliet when she tried to tell him how she felt – especially when she was sad. It reminded the knight that he was sad, too. In fact, one of the reasons why he'd taken to leaving his armor on all the time was that it muffled the sound of Juliet's sad voice. All he had to do was pull down his visor, and he could shut her out.

Juliet must have felt very lonely talking to a man encased in steel – as lonely as he felt sitting in this tomblike room. His own pain and loneliness welled up in him. Soon he felt Juliet's pain and loneliness, too. For years, he had forced her to live in a castle of silence. He burst into tears.

The knight cried for so long that his tears poured through the holes in his visor and soaked the rug beneath him. The tears flowed into the fireplace and doused the fire. Indeed, the entire room was starting to flood, and the knight might have drowned if another door hadn't appeared in the wall just then.

受了前面發展的鼓勵，進房間以後，武士做了一件他沒從來沒有做過的事：他靜靜地坐下，傾聽寂靜。他發現自己這一生，從沒有真正聆聽過任何人說話，或是聆聽任何聲音—風吹過的沙沙聲，下雨時的淅瀝聲，還有溪水潺潺流過小溪的聲音，這些聲音一直都存在著，但是他從來沒有認真地聽見過。他也從未真正聽茱莉亞說話，特別是在她傷心的時候。當她想辦法要告訴他她的感覺，她的悲傷卻讓武士想到自己的悲傷。事實上，為什麼武士老是穿著盔甲不脫下來，也是因為這樣可以擾亂茱莉亞悲傷的聲音，只要把面盔拉下來，他就可以拒茱莉亞於千里之外。

和一個總是全身包著鐵甲的人說話，茱莉亞那時一定覺得很孤單——就像他現在坐在一間墳墓似的房間裡的感覺一樣，他感到自己的痛苦和孤獨在心中湧出。很快地，他也能感覺到茱莉亞的痛苦和孤獨，這麼多年來，他逼她住在另一座沉默之堡裡，他開始嚎啕大哭。

武士哭了很久很久，眼淚從面盔裡的洞裡泉湧而出，把他身下的地毯弄得全濕，眼淚還流進壁爐裡，把火都悶熄了。說真的，整個房間開始淹大水。如果不是在那時候牆上出現了另一扇門的話，武士可能就淹死了。

Although he was exhausted from the deluge, he waded to the door, pulled it open, and entered a room that wasn't much bigger than the stall where he'd once kept his horse. "I wonder why these rooms keep getting smaller," he asked himself aloud.

A voice replied, "Because you're closing in on yourself."

Startled, the knight looked around. He was alone – or so he had believed. Who had spoken?

"You did," said the voice in answer to his thought.

The voice seemed to come from within himself. Could that be?

"Yes, it could be," answered the voice. "I am the real you."

"But I'm the real me," protested the knight.

"Look at yourself," said the voice with a note of disgust, "sitting there half-starved in that hunk of junk with a rusted visor and sporting a soggy beard. If you are the real you, both of us are in trouble!"

"Now see here," said the knight, "I've lived all these years without hearing a word from you. Now that I do, the first thing you say is that you are the real me. Why haven't you spoken up before?"

"I've been around for years," replied the voice, "but this is the first time that you've been quiet enough to hear me."

雖然哭得疲累不堪，他還是涉著水，走到門前，打開門，進了另一間更小的房間，這個房間比他的馬廄大不了多少，他大聲地問自己：「奇怪，這些房間為什麼變得越來越小？」

　　馬上有一個聲音回答他：「因為你和自己越來越靠近。」

　　武士驚訝地四處張望，他不是自己一個人嗎？或是他原本以為如此，那剛剛是誰在說話？「就是你自己。」那個聲音回答了他腦子裡的問題。聲音似乎是從他的內部發出來的，這可能嗎？

　　「對，很可能，」聲音說：「我是真正的你。」

　　「可是我才是真正的我。」武士大聲抗議。

　　「看看你自己，」聲音說，帶著一股厭惡：「半餓死地坐在那裡，披著一身廢鐵，戴著一塊生鏽的面盔，還耍著一把濕透的鬍子。如果你就是真正的你，那我們倆的麻煩可大了。」

　　「噯，你要弄清楚，」武士堅定地說：「我過了這麼多年也沒有聽到你說半句話。等聽到了，第一句話你就說，你才是真正的我。那以前你為什麼不早點宣布這麼重大的消息？」

　　「這些年來我一直在這裡，」聲音回答：「可是，這是第一次你安靜到可以聽見我的聲音。」

The knight was doubtful. "If you're the real me, then, pray tell, who am I?"

The voice replied kindly, "You can't expect to learn everything at once. Why don't you get some sleep?"

"All right," said the knight, "but before I do, I want to know what to call you."

"Call me?" asked the voice, puzzled. "Why? I'm you."

"I can't call you me. It confuses me."

"OK. Call me Sam."

"Why Sam?" asked the knight.

"Why not?" came the reply.

"You must know Merlin," said the knight, his head beginning to droop from sleepiness. Then his eyes closed as he fell into a deep, peaceful slumber.

When the knight first awoke, he didn't know where he was. He was only aware of himself. The rest of the world seemed to have vanished. As he grew fully awake, the knight realized that Squirrel and Rebecca were sitting on his chest. "How did you get in here?" he asked.

Squirrel laughed. "We're not in there"

"You're out here" Rebecca cooed.

武士充滿疑慮：「如果你才是真正的我，那麼，我是誰？」

　　聲音很溫和地回答：「你不能指望一下子就了解每件事，你為什麼不休息休息？」

　　「好吧！」武士說：「可是在睡之前，我想知道怎麼稱呼你？」

　　「稱呼我？」聲音困惑地說：「為什麼？我就是你。」

　　「我不能叫你『我』，這樣我會弄迷糊的。」

　　「好吧，叫我『山』。」

　　「為什麼叫『山』？」武士問。

　　「為什麼不？」聲音回答。

　　「你一定認識梅林。」武士說，一陣睡意襲來，他垂下頭，閉上眼睛，進入深沉、安寧的夢鄉。

　　剛開始醒來的時候，他不知道身在何處，只意識到自己的存在，整個世界好像都消失無蹤。等到他完全醒過來，他感覺到松鼠和瑞蓓卡坐在他的胸膛上。「妳們怎麼來的？」他問。

　　松鼠大笑：「我們沒有進去。」

　　「是你出來了。」瑞蓓卡咕咕地說。

The knight opened his eyes wider and pushed himself up to a sitting position. He looked around in amazement. Sure enough, he was lying on the Path of Truth just the other side of the Castle of Silence.

"How did I get out of there?" he asked.

Rebecca answered, "The only way possible. You thought your way out."

"The last thing I remember," said the knight, "I was talking to..." He stopped himself. He wanted to tell Squirrel and Rebecca about Sam, but it wasn't easy to explain. Besides, he might have imagined the whole thing. He had a lot to think about. The knight reached up to scratch his head, and it took him a moment to realize that he was actually scratching his own skin. He clasped both of his gauntleted hands to his head. His helmet had fallen away! He touched his face and his long, scraggly beard.

"Squirrel! Rebecca!" he shouted.

"We know," they said merrily in unison. "You must have cried again in the Castle of Silence."

"I did," replied the knight, "but how could a whole helmet rust overnight?"

The animals laughed uproariously. Rebecca lay gasping and flapping on the ground. The knight thought she was going out other bird. He demanded

武士把眼睛再睜大一點，掙扎著坐了起來。他驚奇地四處張望，沒錯，他躺在真理之道上，在沉默之堡的另一端。

　　「我怎麼出來的？」他問。

　　瑞蓓卡回答：「只有一個可能，你自己想辦法出來了。」

　　「我記得的最後一件事，」武士說：「我正在和……」說著，他停住了。本來他想告訴他們有關「山」的事，可是很不好解釋，更何況整件事可能都只是他的幻想而已，這件事他還要再想一想。武士伸出手抓了抓頭，過了一會兒，他才明白自己真的在抓頭。用兩隻戴著鐵手套的手捧住頭，他的頭盔已經鏽光了，他碰了碰自己的臉和亂七八糟的長鬍子。

　　「松鼠！瑞蓓卡！」他大叫。

　　「我們知道。」她們同聲高興地說：「你在沉默之堡裡一定又哭了。」

　　「我是哭了，」武士回答：「可是，一個頭盔怎麼可能一個晚上就鏽光了？」

　　兩隻動物狂笑起來，瑞蓓卡笑得在地上喘氣，還不停地拍著翅膀，看起來和之前判若二鳥。武士問她們什麼事這麼好笑。

to know what was so funny.

Squirrel was the first to catch her breath. "You weren't in the castle just overnight."

"Then for how long?"

"What if I told you that while you were in there I could have easily gathered more than five thousand nuts?"

"I would say you're nuts!" exclaimed the knight.

"You were in the castle for a long, long time," affirmed Rebecca.

The knight's mouth dropped open in disbelief. He looked toward the sky and, in a booming voice, said, "Merlin, I must talk to you."

As he had promised, the magician appeared immediately. He was bare except for his long beard, and he was dripping wet. Apparently the knight had caught Merlin taking a bath.

"Sorry about the intrusion," said the knight, "but this is an emergency! I…"

"It is all right," said Merlin, interrupting. "Magicians are often inconvenienced"

He shook the water from his beard. "To answer your question, it is true. You were in the Castle of Silence for a very long time."

松鼠終於喘過氣來：「你在堡裡不只待了一個晚上。」

「那麼多久？」

「如果我告訴你，你在城堡裡的時候，我已經採集了五千顆以上的堅果，你覺得怎麼樣？」松鼠說。

「我會說妳瘋了。」

「你真的在裡面待了很久，很久。」瑞蓓卡再次保證。

武士無法置信地張大了嘴，看著天上，他用震耳的聲音說：「梅林，我一定要跟你說話。」

就像以前答應過的，梅林立刻在眼前出現了。除了那把長鬍子外，梅林全身一絲不掛，而且濕淋淋的還在滴水，顯然武士正好逮到法師正在入浴。

「對不起，打擾了，」武士說：「不過，這是緊急事件，我……」

「沒關係，」梅林說，打斷他：「我們法師都得習慣這種不方便。」

他甩掉鬍子上的水。「回答你的問題，真的，你真的在沉默之堡裡待了段很長的時間。」

梅林總能讓武士大吃一驚。「你怎麼知道我想問這個？」

Merlin never failed to astound the knight. "How could you know I wanted to ask you that?"

"Since I know myself, I can know you. We are all part of each other."

The knight thought for a moment. "I'm beginning to understand. I could feel Juliet's pain because I'm part of her?"

"Yes," Merlin answered. "That is why you could cry for her as well as for yourself. That was the first time you shed tears for another."

The knight told Merlin that he felt proud. The magician smiled indulgently. "One does not have to feel proud of being human. It is as pointless as it would be for Rebecca to feel proud that she can fly. Rebecca was born with wings. You were born with a heart – and now you are using it, just as you were meant to do."

"You really know how to bring a fella down, Merlin," said the knight.

"I did not mean to be hard on you. You are doing very well, or you never would have met Sam."

The knight felt relieved. "Then I really did hear him? It wasn't just my imagination?"

Merlin chuckled. "No, Sam is real – in fact, a more real you than the one you have been calling I all these years. You are not going crazy. You are just

「因為我了解自己，就能了解你。我們都是彼此的一部分。」

武士想了一下：「我了解了，所以我現在可以體會茱莉亞的痛苦，是因為我是她的一部分？」

「對，」梅林回答：「這就是為什麼你可以為她和為自己哭，這是第一次你為別人流淚。」

武士告訴梅林他覺得滿為自己驕傲的。

梅林寬大地笑了：「人不必為了自己有人性而感到自傲，這就像瑞蓓卡為了會飛而驕傲一樣無稽。瑞蓓卡能飛是因為她生來就有翅膀，你生來就有心。現在你開始用心，這是你本來就該做的。」

「你真曉得怎麼讓人覺得漏氣，梅林。」武士說。

「我不是故意對你不客氣，你做得很好，不然你不會碰到『山』。」

武士鬆了一口氣：「那麼我真的聽到了他的聲音？那不是我的幻想？」

梅林笑了出來：「不是，『山』是真的——事實上，他可能比你這些年來稱作是『我』的東西，還要更真實一點。你沒有

starting to listen to your real self. That is why time passed so swiftly without your realizing it."

"I don't understand," said the knight.

"You will by the time you go through the Castle of Knowledge." Then Merlin disappeared before the knight could ask any more questions.

發瘋，只是開始聽見真正的自我，這就是為什麼時間過得飛快，你卻沒有感覺到。」

「我不懂。」武士說。

「通過知識之堡，你就會懂了。」說完，武士還來不及問其他問題，梅林又再度消失無蹤。

知識之堡

The Castle of Knowledge

The Castle of Knowledge

The knight, Squirrel, and Rebecca started out once more on the Path of Truth, heading toward the Castle of Knowledge. They stopped only twice that day, once to eat and the other time for the knight to shave off his scraggly beard and cut his long hair with the sharpened edge of his gauntlet. The knight looked and felt much better when this was done, and he was freer now than he'd been before. With the helmet gone, he could eat nuts without Squirrel's help. Though he had appreciated the lifesaving technique, he really didn't consider it gracious living. He could also feed himself the fruits and roots to which he had become accustomed. Never again would he eat pigeon or any other fowl or meat because he realized that doing so would literally be having friends for dinner.

Just before nightfall, the trio trudged over a hill and beheld the Castle of Knowledge in the distance. It was larger than the Castle of Silence, and its door was solid gold. This was the largest castle the knight had ever seen, even larger than what the king had built for himself. The knight stared at the

知識之堡

　　武士、松鼠，和瑞蓓卡再一次踏上真理之道，這次是朝著知識之堡前進。一路上，他們只停下來兩次，一次吃東西，另一次讓武士用磨利的鐵手套邊把亂七八糟的鬍子刮掉，把長得很長的頭髮割掉。整理完儀容之後，武士看起來也感覺好多了，他感到前所未有的自由。沒有頭盔，他可以自己吃核果，不用松鼠幫忙。雖然他很感激小松鼠的救命法，不過這實在不是個優雅的生存之道。他也可以自己吃已經吃習慣了的水果和草根，他了解到他再也不會吃鴿子、家禽，或是肉類的食物了，因為這樣就好像把朋友當晚餐似的。

　　在天黑以前，這組三人行翻越了一座小山，看見遠方的知識之堡。知識之堡比沉默之堡更宏偉，大門是純金打造的，這是他見過最大的城堡，甚至比國王為自己建造的城堡還巨大。武士一邊欣賞著眼前壯觀的建築，一邊想，這座城堡不知道是誰設計的？

impressive structure and wondered who had designed it.

At that very moment, the knight's thoughts were interrupted by Sam's voice. "The Castle of Knowledge was designed by the universe itself – the source of all knowledge."

The knight was surprised but pleased to hear from Sam again. "I'm glad you're back," he said.

"Actually, I never left," Sam replied. "Remember that I'm you."

"Please, I don't want to go through that again. How do you like me now that I've had a shave and a haircut?"

"It's the first time that you ever profited from being clipped," Sam replied.

The knight laughed at Sam's joke. He liked Sam's sense of humor. If the Castle of Knowledge was anything like the Castle of Silence, he'd be happy to have Sam along for company.

The knight, Squirrel, and Rebecca crossed the drawbridge over the moat and stopped before the golden door. The knight took the key from around his neck and turned it in the lock. As he pushed the door open, he asked Rebecca and Squirrel if they were going to leave as they had done before.

就在那時，武士的思緒被「山」的聲音打斷：「知識之堡是宇宙設計的，宇宙是所有知識的起源。」

武士嚇了一跳，不過很高興再度聽到「山」的聲音。「我很高興你回來了。」他說。

「我從來都沒有離開過，」「山」回答說：「記得嗎？我就是你。」

「拜託別又來了。我現在刮了鬍子，頭髮也剪了，你覺得怎麼樣？」武士問。

「這是第一次你把自己修理得還不錯。」「山」回答。

武士被「山」的笑話引得大笑。他喜歡「山」的幽默感。如果知識之堡和沉默之堡一樣的話，他會很高興有「山」給他作伴。

武士、松鼠，和瑞蓓卡穿過護城河上的吊橋，停在金光閃閃的大門前。武士從脖子上掏出鑰匙，插進鑰匙孔裡。把門推開的時候，他問瑞蓓卡和松鼠，他們是不是要和上次在沉默之堡一樣先離開？

「不！」瑞蓓卡回答：「沉默只能一人享有，知識是屬於

"No," Rebecca replied. "Silence is for one; knowledge is for all."

The knight wondered how the word pigeon had come to mean an easy mark.

The three of them walked through the doorway and into a darkness so dense that the knight couldn't even see his own hand. The knight groped for the customary torches by the castle door to light the way, but there weren't any. A castle with a door of gold and no torches? "Even cheap tract castles have torches," grumbled the knight as Squirrel called out to him. The knight carefully felt his way to her and saw that she was pointing to an inscription that glowed on the wall. It read:

Knowledge is the light by which
you shall find your way.

I'd rather have a torch, thought the knight, but whoever runs this castle sure is clever at cutting down on light bills.

Sam spoke up. "It means that the more you know, the lighter it will get in here."

"Sam, I'll wager you're right!" exclaimed the knight. And a glimmer of

大家的。」

武士納悶，為什麼「鴿子」這個名詞會有容易受騙的意思。

他們三個走進門廊，也走進一片伸手不見五指、深沉的黑暗中。武士在城堡大門旁邊摸索著一般會在那裡的火炬，好照亮前路，可是撲了個空。一座有純金大門的城堡裡沒有火炬？「連觀光導遊手冊上的低級城堡都會準備火炬。」松鼠叫他的時候，武士正在跟自己嘟嚷著。小心地摸索前路，他走到了松鼠身邊，看到在微弱的光線下，她正指著牆上一塊發亮的碑文。碑文上閃耀著：

知識為指引前路之光。

我寧可要一支火炬，武士想著，不過不管經營城堡的這個人是誰，此人對於節省照明費倒是很在行。

然後「山」說話了：「這句話的意思是，知道得越多，這裡就會變得越亮。」

「『山』，我敢打賭你是對的。」武士叫著說。話一出

light crept into the room.

Just then, Squirrel called out again for the knight to join her. She had found another inscription that was chiseled into the wall and glowing:

Have you mistaken need for love?

Still perturbed, the knight mumbled, "I suppose I have to figure out the answer before I get any more light."

"You're catching on quickly," Sam replied, to which the knight snorted, "I don't have time to play Twenty Questions. I want to find my way through this castle fast so that I can get to the top of the mountain!"

"Maybe what you're supposed to learn here is that you have all the time in the world," suggested Rebecca.

The knight was not in a receptive mood, and he didn't want to listen to her philosophy. For a moment, he considered plunging into the darkness of the castle and blundering through. The blackness, however, was quite forbidding and, without his sword, he was afraid. It seemed to him that he had no choice but to figure out what the inscription meant. He sighed and sat down before it. He read it again: Have you mistaken need for love?

口，房間裡就變亮了一點點。

就在那時，松鼠又叫武士到她那裡去，她找到另一塊刻在牆上閃爍的碑文：

你有沒有把需要當作愛？

沒有什麼頭緒，武士喃喃自語：「我想我得想出答案以後，才能再要點光吧！」

「你總算開始懂了。」『山』回答。

武士嗤之以鼻：「我要快點找到路出城堡，好登上山頂，沒時間在這裡玩什麼機智問答。」

「也許你在這裡該學到的，就是你的時間永遠都不會不夠。」瑞蓓卡建議。

武士此刻並不想順從建議，也不想聽瑞蓓卡的謬論。有一會兒，他想乾脆就一頭栽進城堡的黑暗裡，胡亂地殺出一條血路。不過四周的黑暗滿討厭的，而且沒帶劍，他也有點害怕。看來沒什麼其他的選擇，他只有解開碑文的意義才行。嘆了一口氣，他坐在碑文前面，再唸一遍：「你有沒有把需要當作愛？」

The knight knew that he loved Juliet and Christopher, although he had to admit that he loved Juliet more before she began lying under wine casks and emptying their contents into her mouth.

Sam said, "Yes, you loved Juliet and Christopher, but didn't you need them, too?"

"I suppose so," granted the knight. He had needed all the beauty that Juliet added to his life with her quick wit and lovely poetry. He had also needed the nice things she did, like often inviting friends over to cheer him up after he'd gotten stuck in his armor.

He thought back to the times when the knight business had been slow and they couldn't afford to buy new clothes or to employ serving maids. Juliet had made attractive garments for the family to wear, and she had cooked delicious meals for the knight and his friends. The knight reflected that Juliet also kept a very clean castle. He had given her a lot of castles to keep clean, too. Often they'd had to move into a cheaper one when he came home broke from a crusade. He'd left Juliet on her own to do most of the moving, as he was usually of fat some tournament. He remembered how weary she'd looked as she moved their belongings from castle to castle and how sad she'd become when she was unable to reach him through his armor.

他知道他愛茱莉亞和克斯。不過他也承認，在茱莉亞開始躺在酒桶面旁邊，大口灌酒之前，他比較愛茱莉亞。

「山」說：「對，你愛茱莉亞和克斯。不過，你不是也需要他們嗎？」

「大概是吧！」武士承認。他需要茱莉亞為他的生命添加的美。她言談機智，又會寫可愛的詩。還有他也需要她為他做的一些體貼小事，例如在他的盔甲還脫不下來的時候，常常邀請他的朋友到家裡來逗他開心。

他想到在武士生意清淡的時候，他們沒錢買新衣服，也沒錢請女傭，茱莉亞會為家人縫製漂亮的衣服，或是為他和他的朋友煮好吃的料理。他也想到茱莉亞把家裡打掃得一塵不染，他還真給了她不少城堡去清理。而且在他打完仗凱旋回國的時候，口袋裡常常一文不名，他們就得搬到一座比較便宜的城堡去住，他多半都把搬家的事交給她去做，因為他通常不在家，去參加什麼比武大賽。而當她把他們的家當從一座城堡搬到另一座城堡的時候，她看起來是多麼的疲倦，還有因為有盔甲阻擋，她沒有辦法接觸他的時候，她變得有多傷心。

"Isn't that when Juliet started lying under wine casks?" asked Sam in a gentle voice.

The knight nodded, and tears began to form in his eyes. Then, a dreadful thought occurred to him: He hadn't wanted to blame himself for the things he did. He preferred to blame Juliet for all her wine drinking. Indeed, he needed her wine drinking so that he could say that everything was her fault — including his being stuck in his armor.

As the knight realized how unfairly he'd used Juliet, tears flowed down his face. Yes, he had needed her more than he'd loved her. He wished he could have loved her more and needed her less, but he didn't know how.

As he continued to cry, it dawned on the knight that he had needed Christopher, too, more than he'd loved him. A knight needed a son to go out and do battle in his father's name when the father grew old. This didn't mean the knight didn't love Christopher, for he loved his son's golden-haired beauty. He also liked to hear Christopher say, "I love you. Dad," but as he'd loved these things about Christopher, they had answered a need in him as well.

A thought came to the knight in a blinding flash: He'd needed the love of Juliet and Christopher because he didn't love himself! In fact, he had

「茱莉亞不就是從那個時候才開始常躺在酒桶旁邊的嗎？」「山」溫和地問。

武士點點頭，眼睛裡開始有淚。然後，他有了個恐怖的想法：因為不想責怪自己的所作所為，他選擇把責任歸罪到茱莉亞酗酒的習慣上面，說真的，他需要茱莉亞酗酒，於是他就可以說，每件事都是她的錯──連他給困在盔甲裡也是她的錯。

武士了解到他曾經多麼不公平地利用過茱莉亞之後，眼淚就從臉上流了下來。對，他需要她更甚於愛她，他希望自己曾經多愛她一點，少需要她一點，可是他不知道該怎麼做。

邊流著淚，他突然頓悟，他也需要克斯，更甚於愛他。武士需要兒子，好在他老去的時候，用他的名號出去打仗。但這不表示他不愛克斯，真的，他愛他兒子金髮的美貌，也喜歡聽他兒子說：「爸爸，我愛你。」可是，他固然愛克斯的這些特點，但其實這些也回應了他心中的需求。

一個想法突然如閃電般閃過他的腦海──他需要茱莉亞和克斯的愛，是因為他不愛自己。事實上，他需要所有被他從恐龍魔爪裡救出的公主的愛，以及所有他上戰場去保衛的人的愛，因

needed the love of all the damsels he'd rescued from dragons and all the people for whom he'd fought in crusades because he didn't love himself.

The knight cried harder as he realized that if he didn't love himself, he couldn't really love others. His need for them would get in the way.

As he admitted this, a beautiful, bright light shone around the knight where there once had been darkness. A gentle hand touched his shoulder. Looking up through his tears, he saw Merlin smiling down.

"You have discovered a great truth," the magician told the knight. "You can love others only to the extent that you love yourself."

"How do I begin to love myself?" asked the knight.

"You already have just by knowing what you know," said Merlin.

"I know I'm a fool," sobbed the knight.

"No, you know truth, and truth is love."

This comforted the knight, and he stopped crying. As his eyes dried, he noticed the light around him. It was unlike any light that he'd seen before. It seemed to come from nowhere, yet everywhere.

Merlin echoed the knight's thought. "There is nothing more beautiful than the light of self – knowledge."

The knight looked at the light around him then into the gloom ahead.

為他不愛自己。

武士越發痛哭起來，因為他了解到，如果他不愛自己，他也不能真正愛別人，他對別人的需要會變成障礙。

當武士承認了這點之後，一圈美麗、明亮的光線籠罩在四周，照亮了黑暗。他感到有一隻溫柔的手放在肩膀上，淚眼模糊地往上看，他看到梅林正朝他微笑著。

「你剛剛發現了偉大的真理，」法師告訴武士：「你愛自己多少，就只能愛別人多少。」

「我要怎麼開始愛自己？」武士問。

「了解自己知道什麼，你就已經開始愛自己了。」

「我知道我是個傻瓜。」武士哽咽地說。

「不，你了解了真理，真理就是愛。」

梅林的說法讓武士覺得受到慰藉，也就停止了哭聲。眼淚乾了以後，他看到房間裡瀰漫的光線，這和他以前所看過的光都不同，這股光線似乎沒有光源，卻又無處不在。

梅林說出武士的想法：「沒有比自知之光更美的東西了。」

武士看著他四周的光，再看看頭頂上的暗影。「這個城堡

"There's no darkness in this castle for you, is there?"

"No," replied Merlin. "Not anymore."

Encouraged, the knight got to his feet, ready to go on. He thanked Merlin for showing up even when he hadn't called him.

"That is all right," said the magician. "One does not always know when to ask for help." And so saying, he vanished.

As the knight started onward, Rebecca came flying out of the darkness ahead.

"Wow!" she said, all atwitter. "Do I have something to show you!"

The knight had never seen Rebecca so excited. She was usually pretty cool, but now she hopped up and down on his shoulder, scarcely able to contain herself as she guided the knight and Squirrel to a large mirror. "That's it! That's it!" Rebecca chirped loudly, her eyes sparkling with enthusiasm.

The knight was disappointed. "It's only a crummy old mirror," he said impatiently. "C'mon, let's get going."

"It's not an ordinary mirror," Rebecca insisted. "It doesn't show what you look like. It shows what you're really like."

The knight was intrigued but not enthusiastic. He'd never cared much for mirrors because he'd never considered himself very handsome. But

對你來說一點也不暗，對不對？」

「沒錯，」梅林回答：「一點也不暗。」

受到了鼓勵，武士站起身，準備繼續向前走。他謝謝梅林在他還沒有呼喚之前就現身。

「沒關係，」法師說：「人不一定知道什麼時候該開口求救。」這麼說著，他消失了。

武士開始往前走，瑞蓓卡從前頭的黑暗中飛了出來。

「哇！」她興奮地大叫：「我有好東西要給妳們看」。

武士從來沒看過瑞蓓卡這麼失控，她通常都滿冷靜的。可是現在她在他的肩膀上跳上跳下，簡直不能自持，一邊領著他和松鼠到一面大鏡子前。「就是這個！就是這個！」她大聲地吱喳叫著，眼睛興奮地發著光。

不過武士就很失望了。「只是面破鏡子而已，」他不耐煩地說：「來，讓我們上路吧！」

「這不是普通的鏡子，」瑞蓓卡堅持：「這面鏡子不會照出你看起來的長相，而會照出你真正的自我。」

這句話吸引了武士的注意力，可是他並不興奮，他向來不愛照鏡子，也不認為自己長得很帥。但是因為瑞蓓卡堅持，所

Rebecca insisted and, so, reluctantly, he now stood before the mirror and gazed at his reflection. To his amazement, instead of a tall man with sad eyes and a large nose, armored to the neck, he saw a charming, vital person whose eyes shone with compassion and love.

"Who's that?" he asked.

Squirrel answered, "It's you."

"This mirror is a phony," said the knight. "I don't look like that."

"You're seeing the real you," explained Sam, "the you who lives beneath your armor."

"But," protested the knight, looking deeper into the mirror, "that man is a perfect specimen. And his face is full of beauty and innocence."

"That's your potential," answered Sam, "to be beautiful and innocent and perfect."

"If that's my potential," said the knight, "something terrible happened on my way to it."

"Yes," replied Sam, "you put an invisible armor between you and your real feelings. It's been there for so long that it's become visible and permanent."

"Maybe I did hide my feelings," said the knight. "But I couldn't just say

以，帶著點不情願，他站在鏡子前面瞪著自己的倒影。本以為會看見一個高大的人，有著雙悲傷的眼睛和一個大鼻子，從脖子以下都包在盔甲裡。但是出乎意料的，他看見一個迷人又活力充沛的人，有著一雙閃耀著熱情和愛的眼睛。

「這是誰？」他叫著。

松鼠回答：「這是你。」

「這鏡子是假的，」武士說：「我長得不是這樣。」

「你現在看到的是真正的你——躲在盔甲底下的你。」「山」回答。

「可是，」武士抗議，更仔細地端詳著鏡內：「這個人簡直是個完美的樣本，而且他臉上的表情是這麼的美麗又天真。」

「那是你的潛能。」「山」說。「美麗、天真又完美。」

「如果這就是我的潛能，」武士說：「那麼在我實現潛能之前，一定發生了什麼很可怕的事。」

「沒錯，」「山」說：「你在你自己和自己真正的感覺之間放置了一套隱形的盔甲，這套盔甲存在了這麼久，終於有了形貌，變成永久的裝置。」

「也許我真的隱藏自己的感覺，」武士說：「可是我不能

everything I felt like saying and do everything I felt like doing. Nobody would have liked me." The knight stopped short as he uttered these words, realizing that he'd lived his whole life in a way that would make people like him.

He thought of all the crusades he'd fought in, the dragons he'd slain, and the damsels he'd rescued from distress – all to prove that he was good, kind, and loving. The truth was he didn't have to prove anything. He was good, kind, and loving.

"Jumping javelins!" he exclaimed. "I've wasted my whole life!"

"No," Sam said quickly. "It hasn't been wasted. You've needed time to learn what you just learned."

"I still feel like crying," said the knight.

"Now that would be a waste," said Sam. Then he sang this little tune:

"Tears of self-pity end up in disgust.

They're not the kind that cause armor to rust."

The knight was in no mood to appreciate Sam's song or his humor. "Stop with those tiresome rhymes, or I'll kick you out," he yelled.

"You can't kick me out," chortled Sam. "I'm you. Don't you remember?"

At that moment, the knight gladly would have shot himself to get rid of Sam, but, luckily, guns hadn't been invented yet. It seemed there was no way

到處只說我想說的話，做我想做的事，這樣就沒有人會喜歡我了。」話還沒說完，武士就住了嘴。他了解到，這一生他總是過著要讓別人喜歡上他的日子。

他想到所有打過的仗、屠殺過的巨龍，和拯救過的公主，一切都是為了要證明他心地好、善良，又充滿了愛。但是事實上，他根本不需要證明什麼，他的確心地好、善良，又充滿了愛。

「天啊！」他叫著：「我浪費了一輩子。」

「沒有，」「山」很快地說：「你的一生並沒有浪費，你需要時間來學習剛才學會的東西。」

「我還是想哭。」武士說。

「現在哭就是浪費了。」「山」說。接著他唱道：

「自憐淚止於自厭，

此種淚不鏽鐵盔。」

武士現在完全沒心情欣賞「山」的歌謠或是幽默感。「你再唱這些爛歌，我就把你踢出去。」

「你辦不到，」「山」咯咯地笑著：「我就是你，不記得了嗎？」

to get around Sam.

The knight looked into the mirror again. Kindness, love, compassion, intelligence, and unselfishness looked back at him. He realized that all he had to do to have these qualities was reclaim them, for they had been his all along.

At this thought, the beautiful light shone once more, brighter than before.

It illuminated the whole room, revealing, to the knight's surprise, that the castle had only one gigantic room.

"It's the standard building code for a Castle of Knowledge," said Sam. "Real knowledge isn't divided into compartments because it all stems from one truth."

The knight nodded in agreement. He was ready to leave just as Squirrel came running up. "This castle has a courtyard with a big apple tree growing in the center of it."

"Oh, take me to it," said the knight eagerly, for he was getting quite hungry.

The knight and Rebecca followed Squirrel into the courtyard. The sturdy boughs of the large tree bent under the weight of the reddest, shiniest apples that the knight had ever seen.

在那個時候，如果能夠解決「山」，武士會很高興地舉槍自殺。好在那時候槍還沒有發明出來，所以實在沒有辦法趕他走。武士再一次看著鏡子，他看到仁慈、愛、熱情、智慧和無私和他對望著。

他了解，如果想要擁有這些特質的話，他只要收回這些特質就行了，因為這些特質一直為他所有。

一想到這裡，美麗的光芒又再度亮起，比先前更明亮，照耀了整個房間，大出武士意外，明亮的光芒顯示出，城堡裡只有一間很巨大的房間。

「山」說：「這是知識之堡的標準建造格式，真正的知識是不分類的，因為所有知識源自同一個真理。」

武士同意地點著頭。正準備要離開的時候，松鼠跑過來跟他說：「城堡裡有個院子，院子中央有棵大蘋果樹。」

「哦，帶我去看看。」武士叫著，因為他現在相當餓了。瑞蓓卡和他隨著松鼠進入院子裡，院子裡有一棵很大的蘋果樹，粗大的樹枝上低低的垂著他看過最紅潤、最鮮亮的蘋果。

「你覺得這些『辣果』怎麼樣？」「山」說著雙關語。

"How do you like them apples?" quipped Sam.

The knight found himself chuckling. Then he noticed an inscription chiseled on a slab of stone beside the tree:

For this fruit, I impose no condition,

but may you now learn about ambition.

The knight pondered this, but, quite frankly, he had no idea what it meant. Finally, he decided to forget it.

"If you do, we'll never get out of here," said Sam.

The knight groaned. "These inscriptions are getting harder and harder to understand."

"No one ever said that the Castle of Knowledge would be a breeze," Sam said firmly.

The knight sighed, picked an apple, and sat down under the tree with Rebecca and Squirrel. "Do you get this one?" he asked them.

Squirrel shook her head no.

The knight looked at Rebecca, who also shook her head no. "But I do know," she said thoughtfully, "that I don't have any ambition."

武士笑了出來，然後，他注意到樹旁有塊石板，板上刻著碑文：

吾獻此果無禁忌，
願君得果知野心。

武士思索著這兩句碑文，可是說實話，他一點概念也沒有，最後他決定放棄。

「如果你放棄，我們就永遠出不去了。」「山」說。

武士呻吟起來：「這些碑文變得越來越難了解了。」

「沒人說過知識之堡是好過的。」「山」堅定地說。

武士嘆了一口氣，摘了一個蘋果，和瑞蓓卡和松鼠一起坐在樹下。「你們知不知道這兩句碑文是什麼意思？」他問她們。

松鼠搖搖頭，武士看看瑞蓓卡，瑞蓓卡也搖搖頭。「不過我的確知道，」瑞蓓卡說，深思地說：「我沒有什麼野心。」

「我也沒有，」松鼠回應著：「而且我敢打賭，這棵樹也沒有野心。」

"Neither do I," chimed in Squirrel, "and I'll bet this tree doesn't have any either."

"She's on to something," said Rebecca. "This tree is like us. It has no ambition. Maybe you don't need any."

"That's all right for trees and animals," said the knight. "But what would a person be without ambition?"

"Happy," Sam piped up.

"No, I don't think so."

"All of you are right," said a familiar voice.

The knight turned and saw Merlin standing behind him and the animals. The magician was dressed in his long white robe, and he was carrying a lute.

"I was about to call you," said the knight.

"I know," replied the magician. "Everyone needs help to understand a tree. Trees are content just being trees – the same as Rebecca and Squirrel are happy just being what they are."

"But human beings are different," protested the knight. "They have minds."

"We have minds, too," declared Squirrel, who was somewhat offended.

「她説得很有道理，」瑞蓓卡説：「這棵樹就像我們，沒有什麼野心，也許你也不需要野心。」

　　「樹和動物沒野心沒關係，」武士説：「可是人沒有野心會變成什麼樣子？」

　　「很快樂。」「山」唱起來。

　　「我不覺得。」

　　「你們都對。」一個熟悉的聲音這麼説著。

　　武士轉過身，看到梅林站在他們的後面，身穿件白長袍，手裡還拿著一把魯特琴。

　　「我正想叫你來。」武士説。

　　「我知道，」法師回答：「人都需要被點醒才能了解一棵樹，一棵樹自足於身為一棵樹，就像瑞蓓卡和松鼠一樣，只做自己就很快樂了。」

　　「可是人不一樣，人有腦子。」武士抗議。

　　「我們也有。」松鼠有點不高興地表示。

　　「對不起，只是人有很複雜的腦子，想要讓自己變得更好。」武士解釋。

"Sorry. It's just that human beings have very complicated minds that make them want to become better," explained the knight.

"Better than what?" Merlin asked, idly plucking a few notes on his lute.

"Better than they are," answered the knight.

"They are born beautiful, innocent, and perfect. What could be better than that?" Merlin asked.

"No, I mean that they want to be better than they think they are, and they want to be better than others are... you know, like I've always wanted to be the best knight in the kingdom."

"Ah, yes," said Merlin, "ambition from that complicated mind of yours led you to try to prove that you were better than other knights."

"So what's wrong with that?" asked the knight defensively.

"How could you be better than other knights when they were all born as beautiful, innocent, and perfect as you were?"

"I was happy trying," replied the knight.

"Were you? Or were you so busy trying to become that you couldn't enjoy just being?"

"You're getting me all confused," muttered the knight. "I know people need ambition. They want to be smart and have nice castles and be able to

「比什麼好？」梅林問，隨手在魯特琴上彈出幾個音符。

「比他們自己好。」武士回答。

「人生來美麗、天真又完美，還有什麼比這些更好的？」梅林問。

「我的意思是，人想要變得比自己想像的更好，想要比別人好，你知道，我總是想做王國裡最優秀的武士。」

「對，」梅林說：「那個複雜腦子裡的野心讓你老要證明你比別的武士強。」

「這有什麼不對？」武士防衛地說。

「如果你們生來都一樣美麗、天真又完美，你怎麼可能會比別的武士強？」

「試試也高興啊！」武士回答。

「是嗎？或是你老是忙著要變成別的樣子，就沒辦法只是享受做自己？」

「你把我弄糊塗了。」武士喃喃自語：「我知道人需要野心，人想要變得聰明，擁有美觀的城堡，想換馬就換馬，人想要做人上人。」

trade in last year's horse for a new one. They want to get ahead."

"Now you are talking about man's desire to be rich, but if a person is kind, loving, compassionate, intelligent, and unselfish, how could that person be richer?"

"Those riches can't buy castles and horses," said the knight.

"It is true," Merlin smiled, "there is more than one kind of riches – just as there is more than one kind of ambition."

"It seems to me that ambition is ambition. Either you want to get ahead or you don't."

"There is more to it than that," responded the magician. "Ambition that comes from the mind can get you nice castles, and it can get you fine horses. However, only ambition that comes from the heart can also bring happiness."

"What's ambition from the heart?" questioned the knight.

"Ambition from the heart is pure. It competes with no one and harms no one. In fact, it serves one in such a way that it serves others at the same time."

"How?" asked the knight, trying hard to understand.

"Here's where we can learn from this apple tree. It has become handsome and fully mature, bearing fine fruit which it gives freely to all. The

「你現在談到人都有想要變得富有的欲望，但是如果有個人善良、充滿了愛、有同情心、聰明又大公無私，那他怎麼還有可能比現在更富有？」

「那樣的財富不能拿來買城堡和馬匹。」武士説。

「這倒是真的，」梅林微笑地説：「財富不只一種，就像野心也不只有一種一樣。」

「對我來説，野心就是野心，不是做人上人，就是什麼也不是。」

「不只是這樣，」梅林回答：「由腦而生的野心可以帶來美觀的城堡，也可以帶來雄偉的馬匹，但是由心而生的野心還可以帶來快樂。」

「由心而生的野心是什麼？」武士問道。

「由心而生的野心非常純淨，不會傷害任何人。事實上，這種野心滿足自己到某一種地步，還會自動滿足他人。」

「怎麼做？」武士問道，努力想了解。

「這就是我們要向蘋果樹學習的地方。」梅林説：「這棵樹長成一棵壯麗、完全成熟的樹，結出美好的果實，並且把果實大方地施給所有的人。人們摘取越多的蘋果，樹就長出更多的蘋

more apples that people pick," said Merlin, "the more the tree grows and the more beautiful it becomes. This tree is doing exactly what apple trees are meant to do – fulfilling its potential to the benefit of all. It can be the same with people when they have ambition from the heart."

"But," objected the knight, "if I sat around all day giving away free apples, I couldn't own a classy castle and I wouldn't be able to trade in last year's horse for a new one."

"You, like most people, want to have lots of nice things, but it is necessary to separate need from greed."

"Go tell that to a wife who wants a castle in a better neighborhood," retorted the knight.

A hint of amusement flickered across Merlin's face. "You could sell some of your apples to pay for a new castle and horse. Then you could give away the apples you do not need so that others could be nourished."

"It's easier for trees than it is for people in this world," said the knight, philosophically.

"It is all a matter of perception," said Merlin. "You receive the same life energy as the tree. You use the same water, the same air, and the same nourishment from the earth. I assure you that if you learn from the tree, you

果，也變得更美麗。這棵樹就是在做蘋果樹該做的工——為天下人的利益而開發自己的潛能，如果人有由心而生的野心的話也會做同樣的事。」

「不過，」武士提出反對：「如果我每天只是坐著分送免費蘋果，我就不可能擁有一座高級城堡，也不可能把去年的馬換掉，買一匹新馬了。」

「你就像大部分的人一樣，想要擁有很多好東西，但是分辨需要和貪婪是很必要的。」

「你去跟想換個環境良好的城堡的家庭主婦說說看。」武士反駁他。

梅林的臉上閃過好笑的表情：「你可以賣掉一部分的蘋果去買高級城堡和馬匹，然後把不需要的蘋果送給別人，讓別人也得到滋養。」

「可是在這個世界上，做樹比做人容易得多。」武士很哲學地說。

「這完全看你怎麼來看這件事，」梅林說：「你和這棵樹一樣，接收同等的生命力，同樣享用由地球提供的水、空氣和養分。我跟你保證，只要學習這棵樹，你也可以依循自然的腳步，

too can bring forth the fruits that nature intended – and you'll soon have all the horses and castles you want."

"You mean I could get everything I need just by being rooted and staying in my own backyard?" asked the knight quizzically.

Merlin laughed. "Human beings were given two feet so that they would not have to stay in one place, but if they would stand still more often to accept and appreciate instead of running around to grab, they would truly understand ambition from the heart."

The knight sat quietly, contemplating Merlin's words. He studied the apple tree flourishing before him. He looked from it to Squirrel to Rebecca to Merlin. Neither the tree nor the animals had ambition, and Merlin's ambition was obviously from his heart. They all looked happy and well nourished; all were beautiful specimens of life.

Then he considered himself – scrawny and with a beard that had begun to get scraggly again. He was undernourished, nervous, and exhausted from lugging around his heavy armor. All this he had acquired by ambition from the mind, and all this he now knew that he must change. The idea was frightening, but, then again, he'd already lost everything, so, what did he have to lose?

為大家提供果實，同時很快的，你也會擁有所有想要的城堡和馬匹。」

武士惡作劇地説：「你的意思是説，只要往下紮根，把根留在後院裡，我就可以得到所有需要的東西？」

梅林大笑：「人類有兩隻腳，所以不必老待在同一個地方。不過，如果人能夠常常安靜下來，接受和欣賞，而不是跑來跑去地想抓住什麼，那個時候，他們就會真正了解由心而生的野心是什麼。」

武士安靜地坐著，深深地思考著梅林説的話。他仔細地端詳在他面盛開的蘋果樹，再看看松鼠、瑞蓓卡，和梅林。這棵樹和這兩隻動物都沒有野心，梅林的野心顯然也是由心而生的。他們看來都很快樂，自給自足，都是生命美麗的模範。

然後他再看看自己，骨瘦如柴，一臉亂草叢生的鬍子，營養不良、緊張，抱著一身沉重的盔甲而精疲力盡。這些都是他從由腦而生的野心所得來的東西，現在他知道，這一切一定都得改變。改變的想法有一點嚇人，可是，話又説回來，他已經一無所有，所以他還怕失去什麼呢？

「從此刻起，我的野心會由心而生。」他發誓。

"From this moment on, my ambition will come from the heart," he pledged.

As the knight spoke these words, the castle and Merlin both disappeared, and the knight found himself back on the Path of Truth with Rebecca and Squirrel. Alongside the path was a sparkling brook. Thirsty, he knelt to drink from it and noticed with some surprise that the armor on his arms and legs had rusted and fallen away. His beard was very long again. Evidently, the Castle of Knowledge, like the Castle of Silence, had played tricks with time.

The knight contemplated this rather odd phenomenon and soon realized that Merlin had been right. He decided that time does pass quickly when one is listening to oneself. He recollected how often time had dragged on and on when he was depending upon others to fill it.

With all his armor gone except for the breastplate, the knight felt lighter and younger than he had in years. He also discovered that he liked himself better than he had in years. With the firm step of a young man, he started out for the Castle of Will and Daring with Rebecca flying above him and Squirrel scrambling at his heels.

說完這句話後，城堡和梅林同時消失了，武士發現又和瑞蓓卡和松鼠回到真理之道上。路旁有一條閃閃發光的清澈小溪。口渴的他彎下腰去喝水，有點驚訝地發現手臂和腿上的盔甲已經生鏽掉了下來，還有，他的鬍子又長長了。就像沉默之堡一樣，知識之堡又玩了套時間的把戲。

　　武士思考著這個相當奇怪的現象，很快了解到梅林是對的，原來人在聆聽自己的時候，時間真的過得這麼快。他想起以前要依賴別人來填補空虛，那時時間過得還真慢。

　　現在盔甲大部分都鏽掉了，只剩下胸甲，他感到多年未有的輕鬆和年輕，也發現自己比從前更喜歡自己。於是，踏著和年輕人一樣的堅定步伐，他向志勇之堡出發，瑞蓓卡在頭頂盤旋，小松鼠在腳跟旁邊賣力跟隨。

志勇之堡

The Castle of Will and Daring

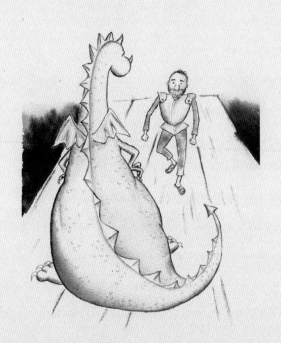

The Castle of Will and Daring

By dawn of the next day, the unlikely trio came to the final castle. It was taller than the others, and its walls looked thicker. Confident that he'd soon pass through this castle as well, the knight started across the drawbridge with the animals.

When they were halfway across, the door to the castle flew open and out lumbered a huge, menacing, fire-breathing dragon, glittering with shiny, green scales. Shocked, the knight stopped dead in his tracks. He'd seen some dragons in his time, but this one beat them all. It was enormous, and flames roared not only out of its mouth, as was the case with any run-of-the-mill dragon, but also out of its eyes and ears. To make matters worse, the flames were blue, meaning that this dragon had a high butane content.

The knight reached for his sword, but his hand fell away empty. He began to tremble. In a croaky, unrecognizable voice, the knight called out to Merlin for help, but much to the knight's dismay, the magician didn't appear.

"Why doesn't he come?" the knight asked anxiously as he dodged a jet

志勇之堡

　　第二天早上天剛破曉，這行奇怪的三人組到達最後一座城堡，這座城堡比前面兩座更為高聳，城牆看來也更厚實。武士自信滿滿，相信自己一定也會很快地通過這座城堡，和動物走上了吊橋。

　　他們剛走到一半，城門打開，從裡面衝出一隻超級龐大、樣子非常嚇人、全身閃耀著發光的綠鱗甲的噴火巨龍。武士大吃一驚地停在路當中，他這輩子也看過不少巨龍，不過以這隻看來最厲害。這隻龍大得嚇死人，不像一般普通的龍，牠噴出的火焰不光從嘴裡出來而已，連眼睛和耳朵都能噴火，還有更可怕的是，這隻龍噴出的火焰是藍色的，這表示牠本身的瓦斯含量相當高。

　　武士伸出手想拔劍，卻當場發現他撲了一個空，他開始發起抖來，用沙啞、幾乎聽不見的聲音，他向梅林呼喊求救，但是出乎意料之外，法師並沒有現身。

of blue flame from the monster.

"I don't know," replied Squirrel. "He's usually pretty reliable."

Rebecca, who was sitting on the knight's shoulder, cocked her head and listened attentively. "From what I can pick up. Merlin's in Paris attending a magicians, conference."

He can't let me down now, the knight said to himself. He promised there wouldn't be any dragons on the Path of Truth.

"He meant ordinary dragons," roared the monster in a booming voice that shook the trees and nearly knocked Rebecca off the knight's shoulder.

The situation looked grave. A dragon that could read minds was absolutely the worst kind, but somehow the knight forced himself to stop trembling. In the strongest, loudest voice he could command, he shouted, "Get out of my way, you oversized Bunsen burner!"

The beast snorted, sending fire in all directions. "Pretty tough talk from a scaredy-cat."

The knight, not knowing what to do next, stalled for time. "What are you doing in the Castle of Will and Daring?" he asked.

"Can you think of a better place for me to live? I'm the Dragon of Fear and Doubt."

「為什麼他不來？」他焦躁不安地問松鼠和瑞蓓卡，一邊躲開怪物射出來的一道藍色火焰。

松鼠回答：「我不知道，他通常都滿可靠的。」

坐在武士的肩上，瑞蓓卡歪著頭，專心地聽著。「從我聽到的來判斷，梅林正在巴黎參加一場法師大會。」

他可不能耍我，武士自言自語地說，梅林答應過他在真理之道上絕對沒有巨龍。

「他指的是普通的龍。」那隻怪物用一種足以力拔大樹，差點把瑞蓓卡從武士肩上震翻下來的聲音怒吼著。

事情大條了，能看穿別人心思的巨龍是最可怕的。不過，武士總算想辦法逼自己不再發抖，然後，用他能發出最大的聲音大吼一聲：「別擋住我的路，你這隻特大號的本生燈！」

巨龍嗤之以鼻，一邊向四面八方射出火焰，一邊說：「嚇死的小貓膽敢口出惡言。」

不知道下一步該怎麼辦，武士決定拖延一下時間。「你在志勇之堡做什麼？」

「還有什麼地方比這裡更適合我住？我是疑懼之龍。」

The knight had to admit this dragon was well named. Fear and doubt were precisely what he felt.

The dragon bellowed again. "I'm here to knock off all you smart alecks who think you can lick anybody just because you've been through the Castle of Knowledge."

Rebecca whispered in the knight's ear. "Merlin once said that self-knowledge can kill the Dragon of Fear and Doubt."

"Do you believe that?" the knight whispered back.

"Yes," replied Rebecca firmly.

"Then you take on that jolly green flame thrower!" The knight turned and quickly retreated across the drawbridge.

"Ho, ho, ho," laughed the dragon, its last "ho" nearly igniting the seat of the knight's pants.

"Are you quitting after you've come this far?" Squirrel asked as the knight brushed sparks from his backside.

"I don't know" the knight replied. "I've become used to some little luxuries – like living."

Sam chimed in. "How can you live with yourself if you don't have the will and daring to test your self-knowledge?"

武士不得不承認這隻巨龍真是名符其實，果然疑慮和恐懼正是他此刻的寫照。

　　巨龍再次咆哮：「我專門在這裡給你們這些自作聰明的豬頭好看，你們以為通過知識之堡就可以所向無敵啦！」

　　瑞蓓卡在武士耳邊小聲地說：「梅林有一次說，自知之明可以殺死疑懼之龍。」

　　「你相信嗎？」武士小聲地回問。

　　「我相信。」瑞蓓卡堅定地回答。

　　「那麼你去對付那隻快樂的綠色火焰槍。」武士這麼說著，然後轉過身，快速地在吊橋上退了回去。

　　「哈！哈！哈！」巨龍大笑，牠的最後一個「哈」字差點燒著了武士的臀部。

　　「已經走了這麼遠，你現在難道要放棄嗎？」松鼠問著武士，後者正忙著把屁股上的火花拍掉。

　　「我不知道。」他回答：「我已經滿習慣享受一些小小的好東西，例如說生命啦。」

　　「山」插進來回應著：「如果沒有志氣和勇氣來試驗得到的自知之明，那人要怎麼面對自己活下去？」

"Do you believe, too, that self-knowledge can kill the Dragon of Fear and Doubt?" asked the knight.

"Certainly. Self-knowledge is truth, and you know what they say: Truth is mightier than the sword."

"I know they say that, but has anybody ever proved it and lived?" quibbled the knight.

No sooner had he uttered these words than the knight remembered he didn't need to prove anything. He was born good, kind, and loving. Therefore, he didn't have to feel fear and doubt. The dragon was only an illusion.

The knight looked across the drawbridge to where the monster was pawing the ground and setting fire to some nearby bushes, apparently to keep in practice. With the thought in mind that the dragon existed only if he believed it did, the knight took a deep breath and slowly marched back over the drawbridge.

The dragon, of course, came out to meet the knight again, snorting and spitting fire. This time, however, the knight continued marching forward. Yet the knight's courage soon began to melt, as did his beard, from the heat of the dragon's flame. With a cry of both fear and anguish, the knight turned and

「你也相信，自知之明可以殺死疑懼之龍嗎？」武士問。

「當然囉，自知之明是真理。而且你知道大家都說，真理比寶劍更銳利。」

「我知道大家怎麼說，可是有沒有人在證明了這句話後還活著的？」

一說完這句話，武士就想到他根本不需要證明任何事。他生來就心地好、善良，又充滿了愛，有這些特質的人不必覺得害怕和疑慮，巨龍不過是幻相而已。

武士回頭看看橋上，巨龍還在那裡用前掌拍打著地面，朝旁邊的樹叢噴著火，很明顯的是在練習。武士深深地吸了一口氣，心裡想著，巨龍存在只是因為他相信牠存在。慢慢的，他再次步上吊橋。

當然，巨龍也走向前來和他對峙，一邊嘲笑著，一邊噴著火，武士仍然繼續朝著牠走了過去。不過武士的勇氣很快就消失了，他的鬍子也被巨龍火焰的熱度燒熔了。他害怕又憤怒地大叫一聲，回頭逃之夭夭。

ran.

The dragon let out a mighty laugh and shot a stream of searing flame at the retreating knight. With a howl of pain, the knight flew across the drawbridge with Squirrel and Rebecca close behind him. Spotting a small brook, he quickly plunged his scorched seat into the cool water, quenching the flames with a hiss.

Squirrel and Rebecca stood on the bank, trying to comfort him.

"You were very brave," said Squirrel.

"Not too bad for a first try," added Rebecca.

Astonished, the knight looked up from where he sat. "What do you mean, first try?"

Squirrel said matter-of-factly, "You'll do better when you go back the second time."

The knight retorted angrily, "You go back a second time!"

"Remember, the dragon was only an illusion," said Rebecca.

"And the fire coming out of its mouth? Was that an illusion, too?"

"Right," answered Rebecca. "The fire was an illusion, too."

"Then why am I sitting in this brook with a burned behind?" demanded the knight.

巨龍仰天狂笑一聲，朝逃走的武士噴出一道強力火焰。武士飛奔過吊橋，痛苦地嘶喊著，松鼠和瑞蓓卡忙亂地跟在後面，一看到小溪，便迅速地把燒焦的屁股浸在水涼的水裡，伴隨著一陣嘶嘶聲，火焰終於熄了。

松鼠和瑞蓓卡站在岸邊，試著想安慰他。

「你剛剛很勇敢。」松鼠說。

「第一次能這樣已經不錯了。」瑞蓓卡加了一句。

嚇壞了的武士從他坐著的地方抬起頭來：「妳是什麼意思？第一次？」

松鼠就事論事地說：「再試第二次的時候，你會做得更好一點。」

武士生氣地反駁她：「妳自己回去試第二次。」

「記住，巨龍只不過是幻相罷了。」瑞蓓卡說。

「那從牠嘴裡噴出來的火呢？那也是幻相嗎？」

「對，」瑞蓓卡說：「火也是幻相。」

「那麼，為什麼我現在會帶著個燒焦的屁股坐在這條小溪裡？」武士質問她。

"Because you made the fire real by believing that the dragon is real," explained Rebecca.

"If you believe the Dragon of Fear and Doubt is real, you give it the power to burn your behind or anything else," said Squirrel.

"They're right," added Sam. "You have to go back and face the dragon once and for all."

The knight felt cornered. It was three against one. Or rather, it was two and a half against a half; for the Sam half of the knight agreed with Squirrel and Rebecca, while the other half of him wanted to stay in the brook.

As the knight grappled with his flagging courage, he heard Sam say, "God gave man courage. Courage gives God to man."

"I'm tired of figuring out what things mean. I'd much rather just sit here in the brook and relax."

"Look," Sam encouraged, "if you face the dragon, there's a chance that it will destroy you, but if you don,t face the dragon, it will surely destroy you."

"Decisions are simple when there's really no alternative," said the knight. Reluctantly, he struggled to his feet, took a deep breath, and once again started across the drawbridge.

The dragon looked up in disbelief. This was certainly a stubborn fellow.

「因為你相信巨龍是真的，火也就變真了。」瑞蓓卡解釋。

「如果你相信疑懼之龍是真實的，你就給了牠力量，牠就可以燒焦你的屁股或任何其他的東西。」松鼠說。

「他們說得對，」「山」插進來：「你得回去一次搞定那隻巨龍。」

武士覺得無路可走，這是三個打一個，或者也可以說，是二又二分之一對二分之一——因為一半的他同意松鼠和瑞蓓卡說的話，而另外一半的他則想待在小溪裡。

武士正在和他快消失的勇氣奮戰的時候，他聽到「山」說：「神賜給人勇氣，勇氣將神給予人。」

「別再讓我猜謎了，我寧可坐在小溪裡休息。」

「聽我說，」「山」回答：「如果你去面對巨龍，有可能牠會消滅你，可是如果你不去面對，牠就一定會消滅你。」

「人無退路，易做決定。」武士說。心不甘情不願地，他掙扎著站起來，深深吸了一口氣後，再一次出發，走過吊橋。

巨龍不可置信地抬頭看他，這個人真是個老頑固。「又回來了？」牠嗤笑著：「這一次，我可要好好地把你大烤一頓。」

"Back again?" it snorted. "Well, this time I'm really going to burn you!"

But it was a different knight who was marching toward the dragon now – a knight who chanted over and over, "Fear and doubt are illusions."

The dragon threw gigantic, crackling flames at the knight, time and time again, but, try as hard as the monster might, it couldn't set fire to him.

As the knight continued to approach, the dragon became smaller and smaller, until it was finally no bigger than a frog. Its flame extinguished, the dragon began to spit small seeds at the knight. But these seeds – the Seeds of Doubt – didn't stop the knight either. The dragon became still smaller as the knight continued to advance determinedly.

"I've won!" shouted the knight victoriously.

The dragon could barely speak. "Perhaps this time, but I'll be back again and again to stand in your way." With that, it vanished in a puff of blue smoke.

"Come back whenever you want," the knight called after it. "Each time you do, I'll be stronger, and you'll be weaker."

Rebecca flew up and landed on the knight's shoulder. "You see, I was right. Self-knowledge can kill the Dragon of Fear and Doubt."

"If you truly believed that, why didn't you walk up to the dragon with me?" asked the knight, no longer feeling inferior to his feathered friend.

不過，這次向巨龍大步前進的可是一個不同的武士——這個武士反覆不斷地向自己說：「疑慮和害怕是幻相，疑慮和害怕是幻相。」

巨龍一次又一次地朝武士射出巨大、嗶吧作響的火焰，可是不論牠怎麼努力，武士身上就是不著火。

武士越向前逼進，巨龍就變得越來越小，直到最後變得比隻青蛙還小。巨龍的火焰熄滅了，然後牠開始對武士吐著小種子，可是這些疑慮之籽一點用也沒有，武士堅定地向前邁進，巨龍變得越發的小了。

「我贏了，」武士勝利地大吼。

巨龍幾乎說不出話：「也許這次你贏了，但我會一次又一次地回來，擋住你的去路。」說完，就在一陣藍煙裡消失了。

「你愛什麼時候回來，就什麼時候回來，」武士在後面叫著：「每一次你回來，我會變得更強壯，而你會變得更虛弱。」

瑞蓓卡飛上前來，停在武士的肩膀上。「你看吧！我是對的，自知之明可以殺死疑慮之龍。」

「如果妳真的相信這句話，那為什麼妳沒有和我一起去面對巨龍？」武士問，不再覺得自己不如自己的鳥朋友。

Rebecca fluffed her feathers. "I wouldn't have wanted to interfere. It's your trip."

Amused, the knight started to reach for the castle door, but the Castle of Will and Daring was gone!

Sam explained, "You don't have to learn will and daring because you've just shown that you have them."

The knight threw back his head, laughing in pure joy. He could see the top of the mountain. The path appeared much steeper than it had been so far, but it didn't matter. He knew that nothing could stop him now.

瑞蓓卡啄著自己的羽毛。「我不想打擾你，這是你的挑戰。」

武士覺得好笑，轉身想打開志勇之堡的大門，可是城堡不見了，一點痕跡也沒有留下。

「山」解釋說：「你不必再學習志氣和勇氣，因為你已經表現出你擁有這兩個特質了。」

武士開懷大笑地轉過頭，他可以看到山的頂端。山路看來比他先前走過的更陡峭，可是沒有關係，他知道已經沒有任何東西能夠阻止他了。

真理之巔

The Summit of Truth

The Summit of Truth

Inch by inch and hand over hand, the knight climbed, his fingers bleeding from holding onto the sharp rocks. When he was almost to the top, his path was blocked by a huge boulder. Not surprisingly, it had an inscription chiseled on it:

Though this universe I own,

I possess not a thing,

for I cannot know the unknown

if to the known I cling.

The knight felt entirely too exhausted to overcome this final hurdle. It seemed impossible to decipher the inscription while clinging to the side of the mountain at the same time, but he knew he had to try.

Squirrel and Rebecca were tempted to offer sympathy, but quickly stopped themselves, knowing that sympathy can weaken a human being.

真理之巔

　　一吋接著一吋，左手換成右手，右手換左手，武士一路爬著，流著鮮血的手指緊抓著銳利的岩石。快到山頂的時候，他發現一塊巨大的岩石擋住去路，同樣的，巨石上也刻著幾句碑文：

雖我擁有此宇宙，

並無一物為我有，

因我不可知未知，

如我不願棄已知。

　　武士覺得完全油盡燈枯，過不了這最後的一關。一邊吊在山壁上，一邊還要解出碑文的意義，這簡直是不可能的任務，不過他知道他還是得試試看。

　　松鼠和瑞蓓卡很想表達對武士的同情，可是馬上忍住了沒說，因為他們知道同情只會讓人軟弱。

The knight took a deep breath, which somewhat cleared his head. Then he read the last part of the inscription aloud: "for I cannot know the unknown if to the known I cling."

The knight considered some of the "knowns" to which he had been clinging all his life. There was his identity – who he thought he was and who he thought he wasn't. There were his belief – those things he thought were true and those things he thought were false. And there were his judgments – the things he held as good and those he held as bad.

The knight looked up at the rock, and a horrifying thought entered his mind: The rock to which he was clinging for dear life was also known to him: Did the inscription mean that he would have to let go and fall into the abyss of the unknown?

"You've got it right, Knight," said Sam. "You have to let go."

"What are you trying to do – kill both of us?" the knight screamed.

"Actually, we're dying right now," said Sam. "Take a look at yourself. You're so thin you could be slipped under a door, and you're full of stress and fear."

"I'm not nearly as afraid as I used to be," said the knight.

"If that's the case, then let go – and trust." said Sam.

武士深深地吸了一口氣，腦筋好像清醒了一點，然後他再大聲地朗誦碑文的後兩句：「因我不可知未知，如我不願棄已知。」

他想到一些他以前抓住不放的「已知」，包括他的本質——他以為他是誰，跟他以為他不是誰；還有他的信仰——那些他認為是對的，還有他認為是錯的事；然後還有他的價值觀——他認為是好和壞的事。

仰望著岩石，然後他有了個很嚇人的想法：他現在為了寶貴的生命而抓住不放的岩石，對他而言，也是「已知」，這是不是表示，他必須要放手，讓自己墮入不可知的深淵呢？

「這就對了，武士，」「山」說：「你必須放手。」

「你想幹什麼？把我倆殺死嗎？」武士問。

「反正現在我們也快死了，」「山」說：「看看你，這麼瘦，連門縫都塞得進去，而且你又緊張又害怕。」

「我已經不像以前那麼害怕了。」武士說。

「如果真是這樣的話，那麼就放手——然後只是相信。」「山」說。

"Trust whom?" the knight retorted hotly. He wanted no more of Sam's philosophy.

"Not whom," Sam replied. "It's not a who but an it!"

"It?" asked the knight.

"Yes," said Sam. "It – life, the force, the universe, God – whatever you want to call it."

The knight peered over his shoulder into the apparently bottomless chasm below.

"Let go," Sam whispered urgently.

The knight seemed to have no choice. He was losing strength every second, and blood was now oozing from his fingertips where he clutched the rock. Believing that he was going to die, the knight let go and plunged down, down into the infinite depth of his memories.

He recalled all the things in his life for which he had blamed his mother, his father, his teachers, his wife, his son, his friends, and everyone else. As he fell deeper into the void, he let go of all the judgments that he'd made against them.

Faster and faster he dropped, giddy as his mind descended into his heart. Then, for the first time, he saw his life clearly, without judgment and

「相信誰？」武士激動地反駁他，不想再聽「山」的高談闊論。

「不是誰，是祂！」「山」說。

「祂？」武士問。

「對，」「山」說：「祂——生命、原力、宇宙、上帝——隨便你想怎麼稱呼就怎麼稱呼。」

武士越過肩膀，低頭凝視下面很顯然是無底的深谷。

「放手！」「山」急切地耳語著。

武士知道自己沒有其他的選擇。在那個時候，他的力量開始消失，抓住岩石的手指也開始滲出鮮血。相信自己馬上就會死，他放開了手，向下掉落，摔入記憶中無盡的深處……

他回憶起一生當中，所有他曾經怪罪過他的母親、父親、老師、太太、兒子和朋友的事，當他向虛空中掉得越來越深，他終於不再責怪任何人。

他墜落入深淵的速度越來越快，同時一陣暈眩之中，他的思想也深降至內心。然後，第一次，沒有評價，沒有成見，他清晰地看見自己的一生。在那一瞬間，他為自己的生命全然負

without excuses. In that instant, he accepted full responsibility for his life, for the influence that people had had on it, and for the events that had shaped it.

From this moment on, he would no longer blame his mistakes and misfortunes on anyone or anything outside himself. The recognition that he was the cause, not the effect, gave him a new feeling of power. He was now unafraid.

As an unfamiliar sense of calm overtook him, a strange thing happened: he began to fall upward! Yes, impossible as it seemed, he was falling up, up out of the abyss! At the same time, he still felt connected to the deepest part of it – in fact, he felt connected to the very center of the earth. He continued falling higher and higher, knowing that he was joined to both heaven and earth.

Suddenly, he was no longer falling but standing on top of the mountain, and he knew the full meaning of the inscription on the rock. He'd let go of all that he'd feared and all he had known and possessed. His willingness to embrace the unknown had set him free. Now the universe was his to experience and enjoy.

The knight stood on the mountaintop breathing deeply, and an overwhelming sense of well-being swept through him. He grew dizzy from

責——不管是別人在他生命中留下的影響，或是讓他生命成形的種種事件。

從這一刻起，他不會再為了自己的錯誤或苦難，而責怪任何人或任何事。認識到自己是因而非果，讓他感覺到一股新生的力量，不再害怕。

當一種不熟悉的平靜感突然充滿全身，奇怪的事發生了，他開始向上掉。對，聽起來這好像是不可能的，但他的確向上掉落出深淵。但是，雖然當他持續向上掉，他仍然覺得和深淵的最深處緊緊相連——事實上，他是和地球的中心相連。就這樣，他繼續地掉落得越來越高，同時意識到他和天地相連接。

突然，掉落停止，他發現自己站在山頂上，而且徹底明瞭了岩石上碑文的意義。他放掉了所有害怕的東西，放掉所有他知道和擁有的東西。樂意擁抱未知使他自由了，現在，宇宙是他的——讓他去經歷和享受。

武士站在山頂上，深深呼吸，一種全面性的幸福感掃過全身。彷彿帶著魔力的觀看、聆聽和感覺四周的宇宙讓他覺得暈眩。

the enchantment of seeing, hearing, and feeling the universe all around him.

Before, fear of the unknown had dulled his senses, but now he was able to experience everything with breathtaking clarity. The warmth of the afternoon sun, the melody of the gentle mountain breeze, and the beauty of nature's shapes and colors that painted the landscape as far as his eyes could see filled the knight with indescribable pleasure. His heart brimmed with love – for himself, for Juliet and Christopher, for Merlin, for Squirrel and Rebecca, for life, and for the entire wondrous world.

Squirrel and Rebecca watched the knight drop to his knees, tears of gratitude flowing from his eyes. I nearly died from the tears I left uncried, he thought. The tears poured down his cheeks, through his beard, and onto his breastplate. Because they came from his heart, the tears were extraordinarily hot, and they quickly melted the last of his armor.

The knight cried out with joy. No more would he don his armor and ride off in all directions. No more would people see the shining reflection of steel and think that the sun was rising in the north or setting in the east.

He smiled through his tears, unaware that a radiant, new light now shone from him – a light far brighter and more beautiful than his armor at its polished best – sparkling like a brook, shining like the moon, dazzling like the

從前，對未知的恐懼讓他的感官麻木，現在他能夠用前所未有的清晰度來感受身邊的所有。下午陽光的溫暖、山間溫柔微風的旋律、塗抹在周邊眼力可及景致上的色彩，都讓武士充滿了無法言喻的喜悅。他的心中盈滿著愛——對自己的愛，對茱莉亞、克斯、對梅林、對松鼠和瑞蓓卡、對生命，還有對他周遭整個奇妙世界的愛。

　　松鼠和瑞蓓卡看著武士跪了下來，感激的眼淚從他眼中泉湧而出。「我差點為了沒有流出來的眼淚而死。」他想著。他的眼淚繼續從面頰湧下，流過鬍子，流到胸甲上。因為這些淚是心之淚，熱度特別高，很快地就熔化了最後一塊盔甲。

　　因為喜悅，武士大聲地哭了出來，從此他再也不會穿著盔甲向四面八方騎去，人們再也不會看到鐵甲的反光，而以為太陽從北升或從東落。

　　含著淚，武士笑了，沒有發覺到有一道明亮、新生的的光芒從他身上放射了出來——這道光比的盔甲擦得最亮的時候更光亮、更美麗——像小溪般閃爍，像明月般皎潔，像太陽般耀眼奪目。

sun.

For, indeed, the knight was the brook. He was the moon. He was the sun. He could be all these things at once now, and more, because he was one with the universe.

He was love.

— The Beginning —

因為，的確，武士就是小溪，就是明月，就是太陽。現在，他不但是小溪、明月、太陽，甚至更多，因為他和宇宙合而為一。

　　他就是愛。

　　—— 故事開始 ——

國家圖書館出版品預行編目資料

為自己出征【燙金珍藏版】／羅伯·費雪（Robert Fisher）作；
王石珍 譯.-- 初版.-- 增訂初版.-- 臺北市：方智，2017.09
　　192面；14.8×20.8公分 --（自信人生；143）
　　譯自：The knight in rusty armor
　　ISBN 978-986-175-471-0（平裝）

874.57　　　　　　　　　　　　　　　106012730

Eurasian Publishing Group
圓神出版事業機構
用心再创新·悉护阅读实践

方智出版社
Fine Press

www.booklife.com.tw　　　　　　reader@mail.eurasian.com.tw

自信人生 143

為自己出征【燙金珍藏版】

作　　者／羅伯·費雪（Robert Fisher）
譯　　者／王石珍
發 行 人／簡志忠
出 版 者／方智出版社股份有限公司
地　　址／台北市南京東路四段50號6樓之1
電　　話／（02）2579-6600·2579-8800·2570-3939
傳　　真／（02）2579-0338·2577-3220·2570-3636
總 編 輯／陳秋月
資深主編／賴良珠
責任編輯／鍾瑩貞
校　　對／鍾瑩貞·賴良珠
美術編輯／李家宜
行銷企畫／陳姵蒨·陳禹伶
印務統籌／劉鳳剛·高榮祥
監　　印／高榮祥
排　　版／杜易蓉
經 銷 商／叩應股份有限公司
郵撥帳號／18707239
法律顧問／圓神出版事業機構法律顧問　蕭雄淋律師
印　　刷／祥峯印刷廠
2017年9月　增訂初版
2024年3月　增訂16刷

定價 270 元　　　　ISBN 978-986-175-471-0　　　　版權所有·翻印必究
◎本書如有缺頁、破損、裝訂錯誤，請寄回本公司調換　　Printed in Taiwan

*The Knight
in Rusty Armor*

The Knight
in Rusty Armor